"Oh, that I _____,"

Renee jun_____ ne

heck out of me _____ so

much when I checked in? Can't you keep your comments to yourself?"

"His beautiful hazel eyes and that thick, tawny hair," she said as she ignored Renee's questions. "From his physique, you can tell he's used to hard work. If I were only forty years younger." Her grandmother sighed.

"And don't forget alive." Renee grinned. "Your death hasn't stopped your opinions one bit, has it."

Her grandmother's ghost floated over to her. "Why should it? My body's dead, not the rest of me. I sure could look at Mr. Callahan all day." She shook her finger at Renee. "And don't tell me you didn't notice how cute he is. I saw the way you were looking at him."

"All right, fine, he's attractive." Renee unpacked her suitcase and stored it in the closet. "I get it, but Gran, you have to behave. No one can see you but me. I don't want the entire town of Garland Falls to think I'm crazy. Isn't it bad enough I see ghosts everywhere and start talking to them without thinking? Why do you think I ended up buying that little Bluetooth gizmo? I'd like to keep this particular part of me between us."

Praise for Annette Miller

"[NIGHT ANGEL] is the first book of Ms. Miller's Angel Haven series, and I'm hoping she will come up with a bunch more."

~Annetta Sweetco, Fresh Fiction Reviews

www.cupid was the 4th place winner in the International Digital Awards Short Paranormal Category in 2017.

An Angel's Heart was a finalist in the American Fiction Awards Paranormal Romance Category in 2018.

Angel in Shadow was a finalist in the American Fiction Awards Paranormal Romance Category in 2020

Praline Dreams won 1st place in the International Digital Awards Short Paranormal Category in 2020

Moonlight and Macaroons won 1st place in the Heart Awards Sweet Paranormal Romance Category in 2021

A Spirited Romance

by

Annette Miller

A Spirited Romance

Cover Art by *The Wild Rose Press, Inc.*

The Wild Rose Press, Inc.
PO Box 708
Adams Basin, NY 14410-0708
Visit us at www.thewildrosepress.com

Publishing History
First Edition, 2023
Trade Paperback ISBN 978-1-5092-4706-6
Digital ISBN 978-1-5092-4707-3

Published in the United States of America

Dedication

For my husband, Brian, and my sons, Scot and Alex.
You guys made me believe in my dreams.

Chapter One

Why couldn't the lawyer have waited to read the will? Gran had only been dead a week and he pushed to get all the loose ends tied up sooner rather than later.

Renee Tate frowned at the bright October day as she watched leaves cascade gracefully down. The sky had no business being as bright and cheery as it did when her whole world had turned a dismal shade of gray. The tissue in her clenched fist had been squeezed into a tiny ball and was next to useless to her now. She stuffed it back into her purse and kept glancing at the door, willing the man to walk in.

She looked at the people sitting in the uneven semi-circle. They had been Gran's friends for years, and she knew Gran wanted them to have certain items. If her appearance was as bad as everyone else's, she must look like an ungroomed poodle. When she got the news of her grandmother's passing, she immediately closed up her shop. Her regular customers understood she needed to take some time off. She'd been close to her grandmother, and Gran's unexpected death had taken a heavy toll on her state of mind.

Renee grabbed a fresh tissue from her purse and dabbed at her eyes. The nights had been hard enough, but the days had been almost impossible. She counted herself lucky she remembered to shower every day. Today of all days, she forced herself to put on at least a little bit of makeup. Gran's oldest friend reached over and patted her arm. She smiled at the kindness the woman showed. In fact, all of Gran's friends had been kind and supportive. The now familiar lump formed again in her throat.

She swung her left leg in a small arc for several minutes before she switched to the right. The lawyer had called them all here at the last minute, and now he had the nerve to be late. Renee wanted this whole situation over with so she could go home and cry some more. She'd lost her parents in her early teens. Her grandfather died several years ago, and now her grandmother had passed on as well. The musty smell of the office had begun to get to her. She pinched her nose to stop a sneeze from coming out. If she sneezed, she might be sick.

The small, cramped office was filled with filing cabinets and overflowing bookcases. The lawyer's desk was smaller than she imagined, but at least the large window behind it let in a lot of light. Of course, the bright sunlight also highlighted the worn spots on the carpet and the shabbiness of the furniture. He'd been Gran's lawyer for decades, and she'd told Renee on many occasions good lawyers didn't need to be flashy lawyers. She'd never trusted those types, saying they seemed more interested in money than helping people.

The door opened, and the lawyer walked in. He greeted the small crowd as he shook hands with everyone. He edged his way behind the cluttered desk and scooched his chair closer. About time he showed up. He lifted up an uneven stack of papers and smiled when he found a large manila folder. He put on his glasses and cleared his throat. The small crowd waited for him to begin.

"I'm sorry to call you in on such short notice, but Esther Tate wanted it this way. One week after her funeral, she wanted her will read."

"Then, get on with it," an older gentleman said. "You've made us wait long enough."

"Right." The lawyer opened the envelope and pulled out a stack of papers. "Let's begin."

Renee tuned him out while he gave away Gran's possessions to her friends. A small bird had landed on the windowsill and drew her attention. She watched it hop back and forth on the sill while the lawyer droned on in his monotonous voice. Even though the window was shut tight, she could hear it chirp, and wiped her eyes. She and Gran would watch the birds land on the hanging birdfeeder outside the back door and whistle with the birds who came and pecked at the seeds.

Why can't I be as free as you, little bird? Why do I need to deal with all this hurt?

"Ms. Tate, did you hear me?"

"What? I'm sorry. I guess my mind wandered for a bit."

He gave the will a quick shake. "I said, your grandmother left you her house, the money in her bank account, and she has a request of you. She wants you to go to Garland Falls, Minnesota, and stay at Warner's Bed and Breakfast. There, you will look for a special oak tree and spread her ashes around the base."

"Oh. Okay. Gran used to tell me stories about Garland Falls, but I have no idea where it is in Minnesota. Do you?"

"I'd never heard of it until I helped her make this will." He pulled a small piece of paper out of the

3

envelope. "This is the information for the bed and breakfast. You can call that number to make your reservation. Thank you all, again, for coming in. I know this is a hard time."

"I'll leave as soon as possible," she said. "I appreciate your help with everything you did for Gran and me."

"I was glad to be of service. Esther and her husband and I were friends for many years. I miss them both very much."

His words tightened her throat again, and she fought back the tears trying to spill. Gran was the only family she had left, and now she was gone. Loneliness held her heart in a tight grip, refusing to relinquish its hold. Maybe someone in Garland Falls would remember Gran, and maybe it would help ease her grief. She guessed she'd find out soon enough. Right now, she just wanted out of this claustrophobic office.

He stood, and everyone followed his lead. Renee shook his hand, then spoke with a few of the people. She made arrangements for when they could pick up the items. They all gave their condolences to her again. She dragged herself out to her car and drove the short distance home. She walked in and threw her keys on the table, grateful for the silence in her apartment. After the way the lawyer droned on, she couldn't deal with Wayne and all of his talk about his work, his clients, or himself right now.

Their apartment was modest and comfortable, but right now, it sure didn't give her the comfort she usually found here. She'd added different colors to break up the bland, white wall monotony. She'd added tan and silver striped furniture in the living room with bright blue curtains. All the other rooms had different bright colors, with a beach theme in the bathroom.

Pictures of her parents and her grandparents were scattered throughout their home. She had asked Wayne if he had any pictures of his parents he wanted to put up. He had one of him and his dad when they'd gone on a fishing trip when he turned sixteen. He only had a few of his mother and several with both of his parents. She'd framed the one he'd told her was his favorite. His mother held him in arms when he was a baby, while his father smiled at him over her shoulder. The rest of his photos were stored away in albums, and there weren't any more of his mother.

She made herself a cup of lavender tea and sat at the kitchen table. It was Gran's favorite, and now she was gone. She'd never again get to do the fun things they loved or have a quiet cup of afternoon tea again. The will had been read, and she'd been given special instructions. Sure, Gran had mentioned Garland Falls a few times, but now Renee wished she'd been more persistent about getting her grandmother to talk about this small town. Gran would always smile and said they'd talk about it later. Well, she was headed that way tomorrow. It would have been nice to know more about where she was going and what waited for her there.

She stared at Gran's urn where it sat in the middle of the kitchen table while she thought about the trip west. Loneliness once again reared its ugly head, turning her blood to sludge. She washed out her cup and turned it upside down on the plastic dishrack. How would she get along without her grandmother's love and advice? She groaned quietly when she heard the front door shut. Wayne walked in and kissed her cheek before leaning against the counter.

She and Wayne had been dating for going on seven months now. At first, his looks attracted her when he walked into her shop. Light brown hair with golden highlights, classic movie star good looks, and he carried himself with supreme confidence. From the cut of his suit, she knew he must have a good job and couldn't be classified as "a bum." Gran had always warned her to watch out for freeloaders. They moved in together three months into their relationship. Now, she had to wonder if this arrangement was a huge mistake. Her friends certainly thought so, and Gran had made no secret of her dislike.

"Hey, baby," he said, making her cringe. "What a day I had today. Picked up three more clients for the firm, and my boss told me I'll get a substantial raise soon."

"Gran's will was read today. In it, she requested I go to Garland Falls, Minnesota," she said. "I'm heading there tomorrow."

"What?" Wayne immediately straightened up and stared at her. "I don't think you should go, at least not so soon. Stay away until you do some research about the area and the people. You don't know what kind of weirdos could inhabit that town."

"Have you ever heard of Garland Falls or been there?"

"Just rumors," he said and glanced away. "Nothing more than rumors."

Renee folded her arms. "Then I'm not sure I understand your attitude. Gran requested I take her ashes there and spread them. I'm going to do it, Wayne, whether you like it or not. I want to. I think we both need a small break right now. And stop calling me baby. I keep telling you how much I hate that name."

"Sorry." His eyes narrowed when what she said finally hit him. "Wait a minute. How small a break are you talking about?"

"The couple of weeks that I'll be gone, that's all. I think we need a little distance right now. I should be home around Halloween." She glanced at him. "We'll talk about where we're headed when I get back. All right?"

"I suppose, but I don't like the thought of you all alone in a strange town." He pulled her close. "Don't stay away too long. I have an important question I want to ask you. I wish I could get the time off to go with you, but the firm is in the middle of some important negotiations. The boss needs me there."

"I know he does. You're an important part of the company. I'll call you the minute I get there." She pushed out of his arms. "Don't worry. I'll be fine. I've got to pack."

"I'll call you, too, just to make sure you're all right."

She pulled out her suitcase and laid it on the bed. Flipping it open, she put in several pairs of shoes and started putting her clothes on top. Garland Falls. The name sounded nice, but nice, small towns figured in a lot of horror movies. Should she put off the trip until she knew more about this town like Wayne wanted her to?

She had told Gran's lawyer she'd leave as soon as possible. No, she'd head out tomorrow, like she originally planned. She'd find out all she needed to know about Garland Falls when she got there. If it turned out to be a haven for creepy people or objects, she'd turn around and head home.

Chapter Two

Renee stepped out of her car and gaped at the woods and the large building in front of her. Her grandmother wanted her ashes spread here? There had to be hundreds of trees in all directions, and most of them looked like oak trees. How would she ever find the right one?

She shivered in the cool October air as she stood next to her car. She stared at the three-story, Victorian home. She hadn't expected Warner's Bed and Breakfast to be so large, or maybe imposing was the better word. The B and B towered over her, and she swallowed hard. Her grandmother's stories made it sound small and intimate, almost quaint. The slate gray porch wrapped around the sides of the home as far as she could see. She shivered again as the setting sun created long shadows across the property.

"This place is nice, not creepy," she whispered. "It only looks creepy because the sun is starting to set. It's nice, and it's pretty, and I'm being completely ridiculous, and there's nothing creepy here."

The white, wooden siding gleamed with new paint. The shutters and trim around the roof were painted a pretty light green. Three light-colored wood rockers stretched to either side of the front door. Autumn leaf garland decorated the entire doorframe. More draped low off the wooden rail. In each window sat a small flower pot with bright red geraniums. Above the flowers hung sprigs of mistletoe.

"Odd mix of fall decorations, but who am I to judge?" She opened the passenger door and laid her hand on the large, golden urn on the seat. "Well, we're here, Gran. I hope I can find this oak tree you mentioned in your will. I have to say, it looks a huge task you gave me."

Renee took one more glance at the urn, grabbed her purse, and shut the door. Once she spread her grandmother's ashes, Gran would be gone forever. She wiped her eyes and headed for the B and B. She climbed the steps slowly and stood near the edge of the porch.

Why did she continue to stand out here? She needed to get checked in and get some rest. Tomorrow, she'd have to start her search for Gran's oak tree. Absorbed in her thoughts and her grief, she almost ran into a man as he adjusted a large, fall leaf wreath on one of the columns.

"I'm sorry. I didn't see you there," she said, stumbling backward. "I guess I'm a little pre-occupied. It's been a long day and a longer drive."

He smiled. "It's all right. Are you checking in?"

"Yes. I'm the new guest."

He laid his hammer on a small table. "Do you need help with your bags?"

"I only have a small suitcase and my laptop bag."

He nodded and walked to her car. She pressed the button on her key fob to pop the trunk and watched him grab her bags. If the man worked here, shouldn't he talk more to the guests? Didn't he like to talk to people? She shrugged and went inside.

A bell sat to her right on the mahogany check-in counter. A small bowl of candy corn beckoned to her, and she took a handful. The dark wood of the counter contrasted beautifully with the light, hardwood floors. Across from the check-in desk, an arched doorway opened into a huge dining room. A staircase with a dark wood railing was off to her right and covered with a floral runner. A small table in the hall held a vase filled with white geraniums, purple asters, and maroon mums.

She smiled a little as she gazed around. So far, so good. Not a creepy thing or person in sight. Maybe this wouldn't be so bad after all. She shouldn't have allowed Wayne to kick her imagination into overdrive. After all, the B and B had a very comfortable feel to it, unlike the rundown motels in some of her favorite movies.

She tapped the bell once, and a door marked "Office" opened. A short, slightly round older woman hurried out. She had a red and yellow marigold tucked into her silver hair. It matched with the muted yellow shirt, dark brown vest, and gray slacks she wore. A merry twinkle lit up her eyes when she saw Renee standing at the counter.

"Welcome to Warner's Bed and Breakfast." She smiled and shook Renee's hand. "You must be Renee Tate. I'm Dee Warner, the owner."

"Yes, ma'am, that's me." She handed over her credit card. "Your place is beautiful."

"Why, thank you, dear. It takes a lot of work to keep it in tip top shape, but if I didn't love what I do, the task would overwhelm me. Of course, I also have some help, and here he is now." She glanced over Renee's shoulder. "Parker, please take Ms. Tate's bags to room 204."

"Okay, Miss Dee." Parker turned to Renee. "I left the urn on the front seat. Do you want me to bring that in, too?"

"No, thank you. I'll get it myself." She watched Parker walked up the short flight of stairs to the second floor. Wow. He was quite the handsome man. How did she not notice when she almost ran into him on the porch? She forced herself to quit staring at his retreating back and returned her gaze to Dee. "We've had a rash of burglaries in my neighborhood. I didn't feel comfortable leaving my grandmother's ashes at home."

"I see," Dee said. "Any other reason?"

Renee shifted from foot to foot. "Well, yes, there is. She wanted me to spread her ashes around the oak tree where my grandfather proposed to her. She said it was here at your B and B. You wouldn't happen to know where a certain special oak tree would be, would you? I'm afraid I might have bitten off more than I can chew with the job she gave me."

Dee frowned a little while she looked off into space for a moment. "We have a lot of oak trees on the property, and some *are* pretty special. My groundskeeper, Parker Callahan, will have a better knowledge of the area than I will. You can ask him." She smiled when he came down the steps. "Parker, would you please come here for a moment?"

"Do you need some help, Miss Dee?"

Dee chuckled. "Not me this time. Parker, I'd like to you meet Renee Tate. Renee, this is Parker Callahan. Ms. Tate will need some help to find a particular oak tree on the property. I thought you might be able to help her look."

"I don't think I'll have much time. I still have to finish the decorations outside of the B and B. Then Mrs. Hall needs me to deliver flowers and hay bales to the town hall for the Halloween party. This time of year my brother always needs me to run a lot of errands for him."

Dee waved away his excuses. "Oh, pish tosh. I'm certain you can spare a few minutes every day to help a guest."

"If he's too busy, I'm sure I can find it on my own," Renee said. She jerked her head around and frowned over her shoulder. "Of course, I'd be glad for any help."

"I'll have some free time tomorrow to help you," Parker mumbled.

"Thanks. I'd better get the urn and go up to my room. It's been a long trip." She turned to the door and stopped. "Is there a certain place I should park my car?"

"There's a small lot to the right of the building," Dee said.

Renee moved her car and sat there for a minute. The house was warm and inviting, but the woods behind the small parking lot held a much different vibe. A low, soft moan drifted to her, making her shiver. She looked in the rearview mirror and couldn't see any movement at all. Again she wondered if Wayne was right and she should've done some research on Garland Falls. She mentally shook herself. No. She was letting the stress of the past few weeks get to her.

She held the urn tight to her chest and hurried inside to her room. Her grandmother's request in the will brought Renee to Garland Falls. If Gran loved this town, it had to be a wonderful place. Maybe, everything would turn out fine in the long run. She set the urn on the dresser and turned it so she could read the small plaque. She dropped down onto the bed and sighed.

Wayne had no reason to be upset about this small Minnesota town. This had been the first time he'd ever come close to losing his temper with her. He hadn't wanted her to come, and she'd read real concern on his face. When she'd asked why, he'd only said she didn't know how many nuts lived here, and no other reason. So far, the two people she'd met were nice. Of course, Parker Callahan was nice looking.

"Okay, enough of those kinds of thoughts," she scolded herself. She dialed Wayne and left a voicemail. "Well, he's supposed to call me tomorrow. He promised."

"Oh, that Parker Callahan is one handsome devil."

Renee jumped to her feet. "Gran, you scared the heck out of me. And why did you have to mumble so much when I checked in? Can't you keep your comments to yourself?"

"His beautiful hazel eyes and that thick, tawny hair," she said as she ignored Renee's questions. "From his physique, you can tell he's used to hard work. If I were only forty years younger." Her grandmother sighed.

"And don't forget alive." Renee grinned. "Your death hasn't stopped your opinions one bit, has it."

Her grandmother's ghost floated over to her. "Why should it? My body's dead, not the rest of me. I sure could look at Mr. Callahan all day." She shook her finger at Renee. "And don't tell me you didn't notice how cute he is. I saw the way you were looking at him."

"All right, fine, he's attractive." Renee unpacked her suitcase and stored it in the closet. "I get it, but Gran, you have to behave. No one can see you but me. I don't want the entire town of Garland Falls to think I'm crazy. Isn't it bad enough I see ghosts everywhere and start talking to them without thinking? Why do you think I ended up buying that little Bluetooth gizmo? I'd like to keep this particular part of me between us."

"I'm pretty sure no one will think you're crazy." Her grandmother winked. "Besides, some of the people here might surprise you with what they can see and do."

Renee stared at her grandmother's ghost. "What exactly do you mean by that cryptic statement?"

"You'll find out sooner or later," Gran said as she faded away.

Chapter Three

Renee propped her head up on her hand and picked at her breakfast the next morning. Her hunger fled as soon as she filled her plate. Having Gran's ghost nearby wasn't the same as her physical presence. A light pressure on her shoulder announced her grandmother stood right behind her.

"All right, all right, I'll eat," she muttered.

The large dining room had trays lined up on a sideboard with eggs, potatoes, pancakes, and bread for toast. Renee wondered if she was the only guest right now. She hadn't seen anyone else and hers was the only car in the parking lot. Maybe more people would be checking in later. Dee came out of the kitchen with a plate of cinnamon rolls and put it in the center of the table.

"What's the matter, Renee?"

"My grandmother used to make me breakfasts like this all the time." She ate a small bite of eggs. "It's so hard without her."

Dee sat next to her and patted her hand. "As long as you have your good memories, she'll always live in your heart. What was her name?"

"Esther Tate. My grandfather was Arthur Tate. She loved to tell me the story of how they met here at this B and B. She had gone out for a walk, and they met up on the road to town. She called it love at first sight."

"I remember them. The B and B had only been open for a few years then." Dee glanced behind Renee. "She must have been devastated when your grandfather passed."

Renee nodded and poked at her breakfast. "I miss them both so much."

Dee stood and took her plate. "Have a cinnamon roll instead. It will help you feel better. I make them with my own special recipe." She winked. "Then I throw in a little bit of magic. Why don't you go for a walk around the grounds? The crisp air may help relieve some of the burden on your heart."

"Thanks. I think I will." She lifted a roll and took a bite. Some of her grief eased, and she felt almost like herself when she finished it. "I've never had a roll this delicious before. I do feel a little better. Maybe I'll be able to find the oak tree on my own." She hesitated. "Your groundskeeper didn't look too anxious to help me."

Dee sat across from her and smoothed the tablecloth. "Parker doesn't say much to anyone, so don't take it personally. I'm positive he'll enjoy helping you. His brother is the talker. The only attributes those two boys have in common are their looks and their last name. Their personalities are as different as night and day."

"I'll try to remember next time I talk to him." She scratched the back of her neck and flipped her ponytail. "I'd better get outside and get started. Thanks for the breakfast, Miss Dee, and that wonderful cinnamon roll. I'm sorry I couldn't eat more."

"It quite all right." Dee gathered the dishes and smiled. "If you see Parker, remind him I said to give you a hand."

"I will."

Renee stood on the porch and looked at the town sprawled out at the bottom of the hill. From here, she could see almost every structure in Garland Falls. The rocking chairs on either side of the double doors were a temptation, but she had a mission to accomplish. Maybe this afternoon, she'd go into Garland Falls and see what this tiny town in the middle of nowhere Minnesota had to offer.

One of the rockers started to move by itself. Renee laid her head back and sighed. "Not the best time, Gran."

"Well then, let's get started. My oak tree won't find itself."

She stood next to Gran's ghost and smiled. "You're still a tyrant, aren't you?"

The ghost floated next to her. "Dear, sweet Renee. Did you expect death to change me?"

"I guess not. I wish you could've given me some kind of clue on where it might be." She put her hands in her jacket pockets. "Standing around isn't getting us anywhere. Let's see if we can find your tree. If we can't, then we can always hope Parker will know where it is."

Gran looked thoughtful for a minute. "Try near a creek or maybe a clearing."

****

Parker loaded four hay bales into the bed of his truck. The drive to the town hall would take about five minutes. His brother had included two bags of loose hay for the kids' scarecrow building contest. There were also a few more plants he needed for the gardens around the Bed and Breakfast. Then there were the Halloween decorations that still needed to be hung, not to mention the items he still needed to gather for the special ritual he needed to hold.

"I don't have time to wander the grounds to search for an old oak tree," he muttered.

"What did you say?"

He turned around and his brother, Lucas, stood there. "Talking to myself," Parker said, and slammed the tailgate closed.

Lucas leaned on the truck. "You always talk to yourself. You need to speak to more people than you. Every person in this town is nice if you get to know them. You have to give them a chance."

"Sorry. I never had the gift of gab like you. I have other…gifts. Those don't make for good conversation."

"I get it, little bro." Lucas cleared his throat. "Anyone interesting check in at the B and B last night? I saw a strange car come into town."

Parker hesitated. Oh, yeah. Renee Tate was by far the most interesting person he'd met in a long time. Her shoulder length, auburn hair, fair skin, and slim figure would be enough to turn any man's head. The bags under her green eyes testified to her troubled sleep. Then he found out she was there to spread her grandmother's ashes. As soon she finished her task, she'd leave Garland Falls.

"No."

Lucas grinned and pushed back the black cowboy hat farther off his forehead. "Liar."

"How would you know?"

Lucas followed him as he climbed into his truck. "Parker, you've always been a pitiful liar. You and I both know it. Mom and Dad know it. Shoot, even Miss Dee and Mrs. Hall know it. You want to tell me about this non-interesting person?"

Parker gunned the engine. "No," he said, then drove off.

Lucas' shop sat about two miles outside of the main street businesses. Parker liked working with his brother at Callahan's Floral Emporium on the weekends. They'd wander the fields where rows of flowers bloomed in a riot of color every season. Those blossoms gave him a certain amount of peace. In the winter, the two of them worked in the large glass greenhouse behind the shop. He sighed. He had time today to help Renee find her grandmother's tree. Tomorrow, more work was sure to pile up.

He pulled up in front of the town hall and beeped twice. Two volunteers came out with flat carts to take the hay inside. He jumped into the back of the truck and handed down the bales. He dusted his hands on his jeans and followed the two men back inside.

"Well, Parker Callahan. It's about time you came in to see me," a cheery voice said.

He accepted the quick peck on his cheek and hug from Mrs. Hall. If an event had to be planned, the stout, little woman was sure to be in charge of the organization. "Hey, Mrs. Hall. Have all your plans come together?"

"So far, so good. Have you heard we'll have a new moon on Halloween?"

He nodded. "New moons are my favorite. Full moons are overrated."

Mrs. Hall laid a hand on his arm. "The lack of moonlight won't hurt the ritual, will it?"

"No. As a matter of fact, it helps. The ghosts who want to cross over are more comfortable with less light." He headed for the door. "I've got to get back to Miss Dee's. I'm supposed to help a new guest look for a particular oak tree."

"I won't keep you. If I need any more decorations, I'll be sure to let you know."

He waved and climbed in his truck. As he drove off, he smiled, certain Mrs. Hall would have at least twenty more projects she'd want completed to make the festival perfect.

Chapter Four

"I'd like to thank you for putting off your work to help me," Renee sai d. "I wanted to start looking for the tree on my own, but Miss Dee said that would be a bad idea."

"You're welcome. Miss Dee insisted I help, so here I am." Parker shrugged. "She's right. If you don't know the woods, you could get seriously lost."

"She said the same thing, and I still think it's nice of you to help me." She looked at the woods around the property. "Does all this belong to Miss Dee?"

"Most of it. The rest belongs to the town. There are signs posted to say when you leave her area."

They walked to the rear of the house. The tree line stood about a hundred yards back from the neatly trimmed lawn. A small, white, wooden gazebo with red and yellow mums planted alternately all around the base sat right in the middle, with a small shed in the far corner of the yard. A birdfeeder stood by the back door with pale, blue-violet autumn crocuses around the base. Purple and orange pansies, silvery-green dusty millers with tiny yellow flowers, and pale pink dahlias surrounded the foundation of the house.

"It's so pretty back here," Renee said, twirling in a slow circle. "I love the flowers. Mums were always one of my favorites."

"Thanks."

She ran over to the gazebo and stood inside. A small bench lined the inside and looked to seat six people. "This is beautiful."

He walked over at a slower pace. "Thanks again. I built it myself."

"You have a lot of talent. It's like a fantasy land back here." She grinned. "Now that I've discovered it, I may never leave."

She stumbled as she stepped out and fell right into Parker's arms. "Sorry. I tripped," she said, as she scowled over her shoulder.

A flush crept up his neck as he set her on her feet. "No problem. We'll start at the tree line and work our way in."

"Lead on."

A man who knew flowers and blushed when he held her? Parker Callahan had to be the most charming, most interesting man she'd ever met. Back home, Wayne always seemed to have too much on his plate to spend a lot of time with her. Parker took the time, albeit with some reluctance, out of his schedule to help her. Would he want to get to know her better? Did she want him to? She hoped so because she wanted to know more about him.

A feathery breath tickled her ear. "Stop it," she whispered.

He stopped and stared at her. "What did you say?"

"Not a word. A bug flew around my head." She frowned as she looked to her left. "It's gone now."

"We can start here. There are several old oaks not too far in at this point." He gazed at her. "Did your grandmother say if it had any kind of special marks to help you identify the right one?"

Renee hesitated. "Gran said it might be near a clearing or a creek."

"It won't be here, then. Let's move a little farther down. There's a small creek called Garland Run. It could be there."

"I'm glad you know this area. You and Miss Dee are right. I'd be lost in minutes."

He smiled a little and walked along the trees until a small path opened up. They stepped under the colorful autumn canopy of leaves, keeping a lookout for roots or rocks. Silence wrapped around them as Parker led her to where the small creek ran.

Renee listened to her grandmother whisper in her ear. The tree could be here or maybe over there. It could be on the other side of the B and B. She thought Gran wasn't trying very hard to remember. Gran was a matchmaker from way back. Renee suspected her grandmother wanted her and Parker to spend a lot of time together. She smiled. Not that she minded.

"It looks like the right area, but I'm not sure." She laid her hand against the trunk of an oak at least fifty feet tall. "Are there more oaks around here?"

"Plenty. We'll head south for a bit then turn back to the house. Lunch time will be here before we know it, and I still have more work to do before I quit for the day."

"Are you sure I can't check the woods on my own?"

He stared at her like she'd lost her mind. "No. It's too easy to get lost in there. I promise, first thing tomorrow, we'll head back out."

Renee craned her neck as she gazed upward. "I wish these trees didn't all look the same."

"They don't. Even though they're the same type, each one has its own personality."

She walked closer to him and smiled as she folded her arms. "Are you a tree whisperer or maybe an elf?"

"No," he said, faster than he intended. "No. I've studied trees and plants and all other types of nature. As a groundskeeper, I need to know what I'm looking at and what plants I'm working with. Not only are plants my job, they're also my hobby. My brother has a florist shop just outside of town. I work with him down there sometimes."

"It's always good when your job and your hobby are the same thing." She smiled. "Maybe I could see the florist shop after we find the tree. I love flowers."

"Sure."

They started off again, and Renee replayed his words in her mind. With his quick denial, she knew Parker had some kind of secret. Could it be as strange as hers? Each oak tree they approached, her grandmother would whisper "maybe" or flat out "no". At this rate, she didn't think she'd ever find the right tree. Who knew there were this many oak trees in one Minnesota town?

"I should've eaten more at breakfast." She sat on a rock and rested her head in her hand. "This feels like it will take forever. Why would Gran want me to spread her ashes, and not leave me a single clue about the tree's location?"

"We've looked one morning. You can't give up after that."

She gazed at him and rubbed her eyes. Was he glowing? No, that couldn't be right. People don't glow. It had to be a weird effect of the late morning sunlight.

Taking a quick look at herself, she noticed she wasn't glowing. Now she was sure there was something special about Mr. Parker Callahan. Questions for another day. With enough time, she'd figure it out. Maybe she'd get up the nerve to ask him about it.

She pushed to her feet. "You're right. There's no room for quitter talk on this quest."

They headed back to the B and B in comfortable silence. As they approached the house, Renee laid her hand on his arm. "Can I buy you dinner tonight? It's a thank you for taking time to help me."

He stared at her hand, then smiled at her. "Sure. We have a diner in town. It's not fancy, but the food is good."

"Perfect. I'll see you around six?"

He nodded and walked off.

Her grandmother's ghost faded in. "There's hope for you yet. You invited a man you hardly know to dinner. I'm proud of you."

"Gran, please. It's just what I said. A thank you dinner."

Gran floated behind Renee as she walked inside. "So, you aren't interested in him? He's much better than what's-his-name back home."

"His name is Wayne and Wayne is a nice guy, but in a different way."

Renee shut the door to her room and sat on the window seat. As she stared at the slope of the lawn, she thought about Parker and Wayne. The two were as different as night and day. Wayne was the complete urbanite with styled hair, custom suits, and designer shoes. Wayne made tons of money as a high-end accountant. It wasn't really his fault he was so focused on his career and wanting to be successful. He wanted to prove himself to everyone, including her.

Parker worked outdoors and wore jeans, a T-shirt, a flannel shirt with the sleeves rolled up over it, and heavy work boots. He was Miss Dee's groundskeeper and, well, he drove a newer model truck and his work clothes looked in good condition. He didn't seem the type to need monetary success or to prove himself to people. His job had to pay pretty well, but Gran always said there was more to life than money.

"You look deep in thought," Gran said, when she materialized.

"I remembered the advice you used to give me about there being more to life than money. I think I get it." She turned to face her grandmother. "Wayne said when I get back, he had an important question to ask me. I think he wants to propose."

"Are you sure? What do you think you'll tell him?"

Renee nodded. "I'm sure, and I don't know what I'd say. Lately, I've been having second thoughts about our relationship. I saw the jewelry store bag he tried to hide under the kitchen towels." She pulled her legs up and wrapped her arms around them. "I should call to let him know I've haven't met any crazy people here yet. Parker and Miss Dee are nice."

"Why hasn't he called you? You did say he would call this morning."

"I bet he got busy and forgot. Again."

She looked out the window and smiled when she saw Parker come around the side of the house. He carried two huge bags of mulch, one on each shoulder. Handsome, strong, and a nice guy.

"You've got a smitten look on your face," Gran

said. "You know, maybe Wayne isn't the one for you after all."

"Maybe not, Gran." Renee turned her attention back to Parker. "Maybe not."

****

The space between Parker's shoulder blades started to itch. Someone watched him, and he had a good idea of who. The urge to turn and look at her window hit him like a punch to the gut. Could Renee be the one for him? He shook his head. Lucas believed all those fairy tales about people being meant for each other, not him. He believed in the ground under his feet and the smell of the earth after it rained. He believed in the power of nature around him.

He ripped open one of the bags of cedar mulch and began to line the flower beds with it. The woodsy scent of cedar always took him back to his childhood when he worked in his mother's garden. He emptied the bag and grabbed the other one. New mulch always made the flowers stand out. He eased a few weeds carefully out of the ground and transplanted them to the woods. Just because they weren't part of his landscaping didn't mean they were destined for the trash. Even little weeds needed love and care.

"Parker, why don't you go talk to her? She's obviously taken with you. She's been watching you this whole time."

The same ghost who always appeared when he wanted to make a point, popped in. He wore an early twentieth century sea captain's uniform. He had a short, neatly trimmed beard that matched his dark hair. His ensemble included a black, Greek fisherman's cap with a gray braid across the top of the brim, a navy-blue peacoat, and his dark gray slacks were tucked into knee high, black boots. He held a pipe in his hand as he studied Parker.

"I talked to her all day today, Captain, and I know she's been watching me. She's nice and I like her, but she won't stay. Her grandmother passed away, and she's here to spread the ashes. When that's done, she'll go home."

"I know her grandmother passed away. We've had some wonderful conversations already, even though she's just arrived." The captain perched on one of the large rocks Parker had used to give the garden some personality. "Renee would stay if you gave her a reason to. You need to stop being so reticent when you talk to her, my boy. You can get her to open up more if you do."

"Thanks. I'll keep it in mind." He rolled the empty mulch bags into a tight ball and looked at the ghost. "Will you come to the ritual on Halloween this year?"

"I might. Could be my year to go to the other side." He winked. "Then again, I might stay to give you some more of my sage advice. I know you can't do without it."

He grinned. "If you say so, Captain."

The ghost vanished as, once again, Parker's cell phone vibrated in his pocket. He groaned when he saw the number. Lucas again, for at least the tenth time today. He knew his brother and knew it wouldn't be important. He'd call him back later. He had to get ready for dinner with a beautiful lady.

Chapter Five

Gran floated by the window, turning to give Renee a big smile. "Parker's here. He sure is easy on the eyes."

"Gran, what would Gramps say if he heard you talk like that?" Renee ran her brush through her hair one more time. "I don't think he'd approve."

"Your grandfather knew I could appreciate a handsome man." She gazed at Parker again. "Just like he could comment on a beautiful woman. We both knew we didn't mean anything by it."

Renee grabbed her purse. "That is already way more than I needed to know. Will you be okay by yourself for a bit?"

"Of course I will. I've met some wonderful ghosts around here. There's a sea captain who tells some wonderful stories, and a couple of lovely Victorian ladies. I'll go have a chat with them."

"I sensed about three or four." She paused. "Can you see if they have any information about the north woods? I'd like to know why it feels so dark or depressing or whatever it is making the woods feel so wrong over there."

"I'll do my best. Now, hurry along. It's bad manners to make a handsome man wait."

The presence of the other ghosts had surrounded her, but none had made themselves known. None of them had felt bad or malicious. She grinned. Like Miss Dee would put up with any ghostly shenanigans. Her grandmother would keep some of them in line, too, if needed.

Renee stared at her reflection for a moment in the small mirror hanging above the dresser. If she knew who haunted the woods on the north side of the B and B, she might be able to help the poor spirit. She sighed. Maybe Gran would find out some information tonight. She ran the brush through her hair one more time and left her room.

She got to the foyer as Parker walked inside. *Gran's right again. He's very easy on the eyes.* Funny feelings cruised through her insides, making her heart skip beats and her breath come out in short bursts. Her palms were clammy and, for a moment, she was back in high school, staring at her secret crush.

His tawny hair was still damp, making it appear darker than usual. Those hazel eyes seemed to look right through her. The faded jean jacket couldn't hide those broad shoulders. He'd tucked his red, plaid shirt into worn jeans, and showed off the tapered waist. Even though he had long legs, he didn't stand much taller than her own five-foot seven-inch height. He shuffled from foot to foot, and she could almost swear he was nervous.

"Are you ready to go?" he asked.

"Yes." She yanked on her jacket and slung her purse over her shoulder. "Let's go. I'm starved."

He opened the door for her and followed her out to his truck. He held the door open and waited until she settled herself in the seat before he closed it. *A girl could get used to this.* As he got in and started the engine, it dawned on her that Wayne never did things like this for her. Most times, she felt lucky he noticed her at all.

Parker pulled up in front of a small diner in the middle of what looked like the main drag through town. Businesses lined both sides of the two-lane street. A hardware store, a bookstore, a cute, little cookie shop, and a general store caught her eye. Other specialty shops, decorated for the upcoming Halloween holiday, beckoned to her to come in and browse. Her stomach growled and, for right now, shopping would have to wait.

He hurried around and opened her door. She stepped out and stared at the diner. In between pumpkins, witches, ghosts, and black cats, fall leaves adorned the windows. Fluffy spider garland outlined the doorframe. They walked in, and she noted leaves of all shapes and colors were taped to the counter and the back of the register. The diner had to be popular from the amount of customers inside.

Parker waved to a petite redhead serving a couple of gentlemen seated at the counter and grabbed two menus. "Hi, Sally. We'll grab a booth at the back."

"Help yourself, Parker. I'll be with you in a minute. We're hopping tonight."

He waited until Renee settled on the red vinyl covered bench seat before he sat across from her. She took the menu he held out and looked over the selection. "You're quite the gentleman, aren't you?"

"I'm not sure what you mean."

"Guys back home don't hold the door or help a girl in and out of cars or wait to sit down." She grinned and leaned close. "Are you from another time?"

He shook his head. "No, my brother and I were brought up to have good manners. My mother would have a fit if she knew I wasn't being a gentleman. She always insisted we know proper behavior."

"My grandmother always said she'd like for decent manners to come back into fashion. I guess they have here in Garland Falls." She paused. "My boyfriend back home never does this kind of stuff for me."

She frowned a little when his hands stilled and he laid the menu on the table. "You're involved with someone?"

Do some damage control, quick, her brain screamed. "Yeah, but I'm not sure for how much longer. I think he keeps me around to make sure he has someone to take to his company's different functions. He says it makes him look good to his boss if he has a date."

"That's not a good basis for a relationship."

Renee sighed. "Gran says, I mean, used to say, the same thing. Wayne's a good guy, but I've started to think he's not for me. What about you? Any lady friend for you?"

He dropped his gaze to the menu. "No. I work too much."

Sally hurried over, notepad in hand. "What can I get for you two tonight?"

"I think I'll have the baked chicken with mashed potatoes," Renee said. "And iced tea and a bowl of tomato soup."

Parker handed the menus to Sally. "Sounds good. I'll have the same."

She scribbled on the pad and hurried off. "I'll be right back with your drinks."

Renee folded her arms on the table. "If you don't date, what do you do in your spare time?"

"Read, watch movies with my brother, dinner at my parents' house."

"Have you ever traveled?"

Parker dumped his silverware out of the white, paper napkin. "I visited a couple of cities. I didn't like them. Too big. Too noisy. Not enough plants or flowers around. I felt a little lost."

"Well, Garland Falls is certainly green. I guess cities are too big and loud." She rearranged her silverware a couple of times. "I like the hustle of city life, probably because I lived most of my life in one. There's always someplace to go or something to do."

He nodded at Sally as she put their drinks down before she scurried off again. "There's more to life than to always be on the run," he said. "I like the slower pace of small towns. I don't want to feel obligated to always have my time occupied."

She paused in the middle of opening her straw. "I never thought of it that way before."

He shrugged and gave her a small smile.

Sally put their plates down and hurried off again. Renee ate in silence as she thought about Parker's low opinion of city life. Had she become such an extreme urbanite she couldn't appreciate the small, simple things around her anymore? Could that be why she stayed with Wayne? Because he liked the same life she did? If so, Parker was right. Not a good basis for a relationship.

When they finished, she stopped him from pulling out his wallet and paid. "No way, Mr. Callahan. This dinner is on me. How can it be a thank you dinner if you pay?"

"You're right. This one's on you."

They walked outside and the stars were just starting to shine in the evening sky. Most of the shops were closed for the night, so she couldn't explore Main Street until later. She walked away from his truck to gaze in the windows. Movement out of the corner of her eye made her turn. A wispy, female figure in a Victorian dress floated a few feet away from her. The apparition turned and bowed her head before disappearing.

"Did you see something?" he asked.

"I thought I did." She glanced to where the apparition had been and shook her head. "I guess it was a trick of the light."

How to explain she could see ghosts and, if they wanted, talk to them? Could she explain how her grandmother had the same ability and helped her develop her own? Would Parker understand or would he think she was nuts and avoid her? As much as she wanted to tell him, she didn't want to take the risk. Better to keep silent and not scare him off.

"Will we look for the tree some more tomorrow?" she asked.

"I can help you in the morning, but I have more deliveries to make in the afternoon for the fall festival." He huffed out a breath. "My brother keeps texting me to make sure I come help him."

"Oh." They crossed the street so she could look at the other shops before they headed back to his truck. "Could I come into town with you? I'd like to look in some of the stores."

"Sure." He paused. "Wouldn't you rather drive

yourself? I mean, you have your own car."

She shook her head. "I don't see many parking lots, and let's just say my parallel parking skills are lacking a bit." She winked. "Actually, those particular skills are lacking quite a lot. I gave up trying to master it years ago."

He chuckled. "Makes sense."

Back at his truck, he held the door for her again and soon they were on their way back to the B and B. He walked her up to the front door and opened it. Why did the night have to end so soon? Her mind blanked on her as she tried to find the words to make him stay.

"I guess I'll see you in the morning then?" she asked.

"Yep. See you tomorrow."

She walked inside and watched him drive off before shutting the door. Sure, she could've driven herself into town, but why do that when she could ride in with the very handsome Parker Callahan? And what she told him was the absolute truth. She wasn't any good at parallel parking.

Her mind drifted back to the differences between the two men in her life. She couldn't stop herself from comparing Parker and Wayne. She hadn't wanted to say goodnight to Parker. Most times when she was with Wayne, it felt more like an obligation or a chore. There were a lot of nights when she couldn't wait for their dates to be done. Both men had good qualities, but the scales were tipping more and more in Parker's favor.

Maybe the time had come to listen with her heart instead of her head. Her head wasn't as smart as it thought.

Chapter Six

Parker rose with sun and took a moment to listen to the birds greet the day. He stretched and pulled on his work clothes. Being the groundskeeper at Miss Dee's B and B had always been his passion, but today, he couldn't wait to get there. He brushed his teeth and hair and smiled. Today would be spent in the company of an auburn-haired beauty. A pounding on the bathroom door pulled him out of his reverie, banishing his daydreams to the back of his mind for the moment.

"Come on, Parker, hurry up. You've got a line out here," Lucas yelled.

"I need to get my own place," he muttered and yanked open the door. "I'm done. It's all yours. I'll be by this afternoon to pick up the next load of foliage for the fall festival."

"Mrs. Hall have the organized chaos in hand as usual?"

"Yep."

Parker walked to the kitchen and poured cereal and milk into a bowl. He pulled a pack of English muffins out of the cabinet. He split one apart and placed the slices in the toaster oven. He and Lucas could go through about three packs of those a week. Sometimes he swore they kept the local English muffin plant in business. He dug into his cereal while he waited for the timer to ding, letting him know the English muffin was ready.

What did Renee do to get ready for the day? Did she have a simple breakfast like him, or did she like bacon and eggs? Did she like coffee or tea or maybe just a glass of juice or milk? He finished his cereal and grabbed his English muffin from the toaster oven as Lucas walked in.

Lucas poured them both a glass of orange juice. "You looked deep in thought for a bit. Care to share?"

"I wanted to run over my list of what I need to do today." Parker concentrated on spreading butter on the warm muffin halves. "That's all."

Lucas slid onto a chair directly across from Parker and stared hard at him. "Nah. It's more than that. What's your actual thoughts?"

"You got me. My actual thought was that you text me too much." Parker dusted the crumbs off his hands and put his dishes in the sink. "I have to go or I'll be late. See you after a while."

He hurried to his truck and slammed the door. The sea captain appeared next to him. The drive was quiet for a few minutes before the captain spoke up.

"You should ask that girl to lunch when you see her today," the captain said.

"I plan to." He turned right onto Main Street, giving small waves to people who greeted him. "Renee said her grandmother acted like a matchmaker. Are you trying your hand at it now? I mean, you've never tried to match me up with anyone before."

The captain chuckled. "Now why would I do that to you, my boy? I don't like to interfere in your personal life."

"I wouldn't put it past you or her." Parker turned

right on Main Street. "And you interfere more often than not."

The captain stroked his beard. "Only when you need a push in the right direction.'

Parker frowned. "Doesn't someone else need you to haunt them for a bit? Maybe you should go check."

The captain laughed as he faded away.

He drove toward the B and B. He had no desire to tell Lucas what his thoughts were. The brothers usually shared everything, but not this time. Even with his recent marriage, Lucas could still smooth talk any girl he met. Parker decided he'd keep the secret of Renee Tate all to himself.

****

Renee yawned and stretched. A quick glance at the clock showed five after six in the morning. She rolled over and groaned as she pulled the pillow over her head. She tried her best to ignore the infernal device as it counted down the minutes until it would make its obnoxious beep, forcing her to get up. She closed her eyes and pretended to sleep. When she looked at the clock again, certain it had been a half an hour, only five minutes had gone by. She gave in and threw the covers off.

She steamed herself in the shower and walked out of the bathroom. She allowed Parker to fill her thoughts while she dried her hair. She laid out jeans, a T-shirt, a heavy sweater, and thicker socks than yesterday. Now that she knew the terrain, she'd be better prepared. Her feet were still achy from the hike through the woods the day before. She never should have worn the thin tennis shoes she'd decided on.

"Good morning, dear," Gran said when she

appeared.

"Hi, Gran." Renee dressed quickly before pulling on her socks. "Did you meet any nice ghosts last night?"

Her gran's ghost gave the impression she sat on the bed. "I met a nice couple and a very sweet girl who said she saw you in town. She said it looked like you and Parker got along very well. I had such an enjoyable evening talking to them and the sea captain and a couple of lovely Victorian ladies."

"Now you have ghosts spying on me?" Renee smiled. "You sneak."

"Would I do that?" Gran laid a hand over her heart. "Heavens, no. She wanted to see if Parker had gotten some items he needed for something special and happened to see you two. She knew she had to tell me, since we are related."

Renee laughed. "Of course she did. He'll be here today to help me look around for your tree some more. I hope we find it soon. I can't keep my shop back east closed for longer than two weeks. Are you sure you can't remember the exact location?"

"It's been over fifty years since the last time I saw it. You'll have to bear with me." Her grandmother hesitated before she answered. "I don't think I'm supposed to cross over yet. Even if we do find it today or tomorrow, I believe I'm supposed to wait for a certain day."

Renee sat on the bed to tie her boots. "Did the other ghosts tell you that?"

"Yes." Gran got up and gave the impression that she paced. "They said there's a ritual to be performed to open the gateway to the afterlife. I think we have to wait for the right time. When you spread my ashes, I don't want you to have any problems."

"You know I'll do whatever you want me to, Gran. You tell me when, and that's when we'll do it." She paused. "Do you think Gramps will come for you?"

"He promised me he would." She floated to the window and looked out. "I believe he'll be there. Not once in our fifty-two years of marriage did he ever let me down."

"I hope I have that kind of marriage when I find my own Mr. Right." Renee paced at the foot of the bed. "Did you find out what's wrong with the woods? I can sense some type of entity, but I don't know if it's bad or maybe just a melancholy ghost. The night I arrived, I could hear someone or something groan. I think the woods are hiding something. I wish I knew what it could be."

"No one mentioned a dark presence to me. I'll ask around, though, if it will help you." Gran floated over to the door. "You'd better hustle if you don't want to be late."

Renee hurried downstairs to get some breakfast. That annoying lump had formed in her throat again. After she'd spread the ashes, Gran would be gone forever. She needed to resign herself to her grandmother's wishes. It wouldn't be right to keep her from the peace she deserved.

Dee placed a tray full of warm cinnamon rolls on the table. "Good morning, Renee. Do you have a better appetite today?"

"Yes, thank you." Renee inhaled. "Those smell delicious."

"Help yourself. I've got to get more homemade

bread for toast."

Renee filled a plate with eggs, bacon, and some fried potatoes. She popped two pieces of bread in the toaster and took her plate to the table. She got her toast and smeared a lot of butter on both slices. Her vacation rules were in effect. No more diets until she arrived back in her apartment.

"Did you get enough to eat?" Dee asked, when Renee swallowed her last bite.

"Yes, thank you." Renee patted her stomach. "I guess all the fresh air here has restored my appetite."

A ding sounded from the kitchen. "Excuse me for a moment."

"Parker's on his way, and he seems to be driving faster than usual," Gran whispered. "I think he's excited to see you again."

"He might just be late for work. Did you consider that option?" She glanced over her shoulder and frowned when her grandmother smiled. "I hope we can find the oak tree today."

"You should ask him out again." Gran blew a lock of Renee's hair in her face. "You don't want him to get away."

"He's not going anywhere," Renee hissed. She frowned. After she spread the ashes, she'd be going somewhere. She'd be going home.

"Did you say something, dear?" Dee said, when she came out of the kitchen carrying a tray of warm bread slices.

Renee smiled and shrugged. The trip home didn't sound so appealing anymore.

Dee looked past Renee's shoulder and smiled, as a twinkle lit her eyes. She nodded, as if she agreed with someone. Could Miss Dee see and hear her grandmother? Maybe she wasn't alone in her ability to communicate with ghosts. If so, it was possible Dee had heard everything Gran had said to her.

The front door opened, and Parker walked into the dining room. "Hi, everyone."

"Hi, Parker," Renee said. "Thanks again for the help yesterday. I really appreciate it."

"My pleasure. Miss Dee, could I start work a little later today?"

"Not at all. Since a guest requires your help, that constitutes as work. You can tend to the grounds this afternoon. Do you have to take any deliveries to the festival?"

"A few. I told Renee I'd take her into town when I go."

"Is that a fact?" Dee smiled at her, as she though she knew the answer. "Renee, do you think you'll like our little town? After all, you're quite the city girl."

Renee nodded. "I believe so. I looked in some of the shops last night when we went to dinner. I'm anxious to explore inside all the stores. I can't wait to see what they have to offer."

"I'm sure you'll find some items you might like." Dee stacked the dirty plates. "Now, shoo, you two. You'd better hit the trails, and I have my own work to get done."

They walked outside, and Renee took a deep breath. "Even the air here smells better than the city."

"It helps we don't have a lot of traffic."

"Miss Dee sure had you pegged," she said. "You don't say much at all, do you?"

He shrugged. "No need. We'll head north today."

They started off across the lawn on the right side of the house. Renee shivered as the shade from the trees penetrated her clothes and seeped into her bones. Heaviness in the air clung to her skin, the damp air raising goosebumps on her arms under her heavy sweater. Her grandmother pressed closer to her, and she in turn moved closer to Parker, holding his arm.

"Do the woods feel, I don't know, depressing somehow?"

He nodded and looked down at her hand on his arm. "This part of the woods has a sad history."

She stepped away and waited for him to continue. When he didn't, she prompted him. "What happened here?"

"A young mother ran away from her husband. She had her child with her. The husband found them, and it didn't end well for her. He took their child, and the story goes her ghost still searches for the baby."

"That's awful."

"Yeah. I hope one day I'll be able to..." He stopped. "I mean, I hope she'll be able to find peace."

Curious choice of words, he'd started to say. Is it possible she and Parker shared the same secret? Could he also see and talk to ghosts? She shoved that thought to the back of her mind. The mystery in the north woods needed to be solved first. Maybe while she shopped in town this afternoon, she'd try to find out more about the woman. Maybe she'd be able to bring her the peace Parker wished for her.

At every tree, her grandmother said no. Renee hoped they'd find it today, but after more than an hour of searching, they still had no luck. "We have to find the oak tree soon, or we'll run out of property."

"Could your grandmother have been mistaken about the town where her tree is?" Parker asked. "There are other small towns like this one nearby. They all look alike."

Renee shook her head. "Her will said specifically it was here in Garland Falls." She sighed. "I guess our one option at this point is to search until we find it."

"I guess so."

As much as Renee wanted to find the tree and give her grandmother peace, she'd hate to have this time with Parker end.

Chapter Seven

"Can I buy you lunch this time?" Parker said as they climbed the few steps to the B and B's porch.

There went those fluttery little somersaults in her stomach again, sending tiny shivers down her spine. "Sure, if it wouldn't make you late for your work."

"It's okay. There's advantages to being able to set my own hours." He hesitated, and she saw the sea captain's ghost nudge him. "Miss Dee knows I have to eat, and she wouldn't want you to go hungry."

"Then, yes. Lunch would be great. Let me wash up really quick."

Renee walked into the house, then ran up to her room. She pulled off the heavy sweater and T-shirt. Her hands trembled as she untied her boots and yanked off the thick socks. She grabbed one of the two nice shirts she'd brought and put on her flats. Her jeans looked okay after she brushed off the few leaves clinging to her legs. She only had to neaten up her hair, and presto, ready for lunch with a handsome man.

"What's your hurry, dear?" Gran said when she appeared. She winked and grinned. "As if I didn't know."

Renee fluffed her hair a little. "Parker asked me to have lunch with him."

"Do tell."

"Gran, are you up to something?" She stared at her

grandmother, who tried to look innocent. "Yep. I know that look in your eyes. You're up to something. I never could stop you from matchmaking, could I?"

"No, and you never will. At least, not until you find the right man who makes you happy." Her grandmother started to fade. "Have a good time."

Renee took a shaky breath to calm her racing heart and walked with a sereneness she didn't feel down the stairs. "I'm ready. Let's go."

Parker made her want to constantly giggle like a teenager. She never got this flustered with her previous boyfriends, and Wayne had never given her a fluttery stomach. How could Parker Callahan make her insides go all wobbly? She'd known him precisely two days. Whatever it could be, she liked it.

They went back to the diner and found it as busy as ever. This time, they sat at the counter and ordered sandwiches. After several attempts to talk over the loud voices and the clatter of silverware, they gave up on having any kind of conversation. They ate quickly and Parker paid the check.

"Wow, we made it right before the rush," she said as they pushed their way outside through the people trying to get in. "Is it always like this?"

"Just between eleven and one. The pizzeria on the next street over is just as busy." He walked over to his truck. "I have deliveries to make for my brother. When you're ready to go back, wait for me here on Main Street."

"How will you know what time to come get me?"

He climbed in the cab and leaned out the window. "It's on my route from my brother's shop and nursery to the B and B. I'll see you."

She smiled. "Sounds like a plan. I'll see you here later."

Renee waved as he drove off. What should she do first? The store fronts enticed her to come look, but she wanted to know more about the woman in the woods. She walked toward the town circle to look for the library or historical society. Next to the town hall, she found the library. Finding information on the woman would be easier if she knew what year the incident happened. She squared her shoulders. No matter. She could do research with the best of them.

She stepped inside and took a deep breath. The wonderful, indescribable smell of old books filled her senses. Libraries and bookstores always had that distinct smell. Gran had told her books held the aroma of undiscovered worlds and hidden knowledge, of love lost and love found. She wiped the corner of her eye. This would be yet another pastime she'd never get to do with her grandmother again.

Gran appeared at her side. "Quit being maudlin, Renee. You came here for a purpose."

Renee clamped a hand over her mouth and swallowed her shriek. "Gran, you scared the heck out of me. Stop it," she said in a harsh whisper. She took a deep breath and let it out. "You're right, though. Let's start at the information desk. They may have an idea of where we should look first."

Renee's greeting faltered as she watched two ghosts behind the librarian argue about how the current editions of the newspapers should be filed. "Excuse me," she said. "I want to find some information about a tragedy in the woods to the north of Warner's Bed and Breakfast."

"The historical society would know more about it."

"Great. Can you tell me how to find them?"

He pointed to the stairs. "They occupy the whole top story. Go on up. I'm sure they can help you with anything you want to know."

"Thank you."

As Renee climbed the stairs, she saw more ghosts flitting around. "I didn't know so many ghosts could occupy the same place at the same time," she said, keeping her voice low. "Why do think they're hanging around?"

"Book lovers will always be near the books they loved in life. I'm sure that's their reason for staying here. Maybe you should talk to them and find out for sure." Her grandmother chuckled. "I suspect you'll learn more than you wanted to know about ghosts before your trip is over. You need to interact with the spirit world more. You have the gift. You should make some use of it."

She scowled. "Thanks, Gran. I'll take it under advisement."

At the top of the stairs, a plaque stated she'd found the Garland Falls Historical Society. Renee hoped she could get some answers here. She walked over to an attractive thin, older woman with salt and pepper hair, standing at a small desk. The woman turned around and removed her wire framed glasses.

"May I help you?"

"Hi. My name is Renee Tate. I wonder if you could answer a few questions for me about the property around the Warner Bed and Breakfast."

The woman stared hard at her. "I bet you want to know about the Lily McGee murder."

"How did you know?"

She folded her arms and stood there, looking like she was ready for battle. "It's the one story anyone wants to hear about when they come up here. Why do you want to know? If you're a reporter, I won't tell you one word. That poor woman's name has been the subject of speculation for far too long. You need to let her rest in peace."

"I promise I'm not here for any sensational reason." She swallowed, trying to moisten her suddenly dry throat. "I'm staying at the bed and breakfast. Parker Callahan mentioned it to me when we were in the woods. He offered to help me find a specific oak tree so I can spread my grandmother's ashes. When I sensed a strangeness in the woods, he told me what happened."

At the mention of Parker's name, the woman's hard stare softened. "If Parker told you, then I'll recount the tale."

"Do you know him?"

The woman stood off to the side and pointed to the name plate on her desk. Sara Callahan. "You could say that. He's my youngest son."

"It's nice to meet you, Mrs. Callahan. I want to know the story so maybe I can figure out how to bring her poor spirit peace." Renee shot a look at Sara, who raised her eyebrows, a ghost of a smile on her lips. "I mean, I'm an amateur ghost hunter. I try to help ghosts."

"I see."

Why did Renee think Sara didn't believe her lame cover story for one minute? No matter. As long as she could find out what happened to Lily McGee, she'd let Sara believe anything about her she wanted.

She led Renee over to a glass case with several newspaper articles in it. Renee fidgeted under the woman's gaze. She felt her grandmother's hand on her shoulder and tried to quiet her nervousness. Sara smiled, giving Renee the impression she had passed some sort of test.

"This is Garland Falls' only major crime," she said. "The townspeople never cared for Lily's husband. It's rumored he had a vicious temper and started fights with almost everyone he met. People always said the man had badness inside."

Renee stared at the articles, her gaze lingering on the picture of Lily's husband. Edmund McGee didn't look like any kind of romantic figure. Heavy brows, deep set eyes, and a scowl to scare anyone made her believe he had violence inside him. She stared harder at Edmund's picture. He looked vaguely familiar, but she was sure she'd remember a scowl that fierce.

Poor Lily. The only picture of her was fuzzy and out of focus. Renee could still make out her thin and frail appearance. How did such a delicate woman end up with such a man? How could her parents let her? Did they know about him and his temper? Why didn't they try to save her?

"What happened?"

"Most of the story is speculation." Sara gazed at the articles. "The version I was told is this. He'd been over in the next town, drinking and carousing with his friends. When he came home, he saw Lily had packed a suitcase. She told him she decided to take their child and leave. He didn't love her or their baby so she would let him live his life the way he wanted. She ran, he followed, and the rest is too terrible to talk about."

"What happened to the baby?"

"Some say the fairies took the child. That they raised him or her as one of their own until the child could make its way in the mortal world. Others say Lily's husband disposed of the child somewhere outside of town."

Renee gazed at the woman. "What do you think?"

She smiled. "I'd like to think the fairies took the baby. If so, I hope the child found happiness in their realm."

"I hope so, too." Renee shook Sara's hand. "Thank you for telling me. I'd better go. I need to buy a few items before I return to Miss Dee's. Parker will be picking me up soon. I hope you'll let me come here again. I bet this town has a fascinating history."

"I have all sorts of stories I could tell you." She walked Renee to the door. "Come back any time. I'll be glad to have you."

Renee stepped out on Main Street, the tragic story not far from her thoughts. She stopped and caressed the petals of a rose bush outside of a candle shop. "I hope the fairies did rescue your baby, Lily. I hope you'll talk to me so I can help you."

She walked into Mac's General Store. Wooden floorboards creaked under her feet and the salty, buttery scent of popcorn filled the air. She picked up a basket and wandered through the store. She turned to go down another aisle and stopped when a tall man stood there, staring at her.

His long brown hair was beginning to silver, and he'd pulled it back in a ponytail. He had muscular arms and wore a black apron, the pockets stuffed with pens, stickers, and small pads of paper. His blue eyes sparkled when he smiled as he walked over to her and shook her hand.

"I've never seen you here before," he said. "I'm Mac. Welcome to my place. Are you new in town or here for a quick visit?"

"Renee Tate." She swallowed hard. "I've got a room at Warner's for a couple of weeks. I'm on a kind of vacation. I'm here to spread my grandmother's ashes."

"Sorry to hear about your loss. Up at Warner's, eh?" He rubbed his chin. "You know Parker Callahan and his brother Lucas?"

"I know Parker. I haven't met his brother yet."

The man nodded toward the door. "Well, now's your chance. Howdy, Lucas. What can I get for you today?"

"Hey, Mac. I ran out of ties for the plant stakes. I'm not due for a supply delivery for another couple of days. You have any on hand?" Lucas stopped when he saw Renee. "Hello. I'm Lucas Callahan, and you are?"

"Renee Tate. I know your brother. Miss Dee asked him to help me out with a small task."

Lucas took her basket and accompanied her as she walked through the store. "I can't believe he lied to me. I asked him if anyone interesting had checked in up there and he said no."

Mac laughed. "Better rein it in, Lucas. Don't make me tell your wife what you're up to when she's out of town."

Lucas grinned at him. "Aw, Blair knows she's the only woman in my life. I just want to be polite to our new guest."

"Thank you for the help, but I really have to go."

Renee took back her basket and bit her lip, trying hard not to laugh. It appeared Lucas considered himself a real ladies' man. Even if he wasn't married, he'd have no chance with her. Definitely not her type. "I need to pay for my stuff and go wait for Parker. He should be here any time now. And I'd love to meet your wife. Does she know what a charmer you are?"

"Of course." He winked. "Why do you think she married me? She couldn't resist my sparkling personality."

Lucas shivered and frowned over his shoulder. Renee covered her mouth as her shoulders shook with hidden laughter. Her grandmother loved Parker but didn't seem quite so enamored of Lucas. She couldn't understand why. Lucas had the same tawny color hair, but he had light green eyes. The brothers had the same muscular build, broad shoulders, tapered waist, and long legs. However, Lucas wore a black cowboy hat, talked quite a bit, and was a huge flirt.

Lucas took the plant ties Mac handed to him. "If you want some real conversation, I could tell you a lot about the town and show you around. I'm sure you've noticed Parker doesn't say a whole lot."

"I've noticed, but I don't mind." Renee put the basket by the register. She slid her credit card, signed the card reader, and grabbed her bag. "I have to go. It was nice to meet you."

She hurried outside and waved at Parker when she saw his truck turn the corner. She jumped in and breathed a sigh of relief. She glanced at him when he didn't go right away.

"What?" She hooked her seat belt and sat back. "I'm ready if you are."

He frowned. "Are you okay?"

She nodded. "I'm fine. I met your brother in the general store."

He continued to stare at her. "Did he do or say anything inappropriate? You want me to talk to him? You never know what kind of nonsense will come out of his mouth."

"No, he was polite. I just think he's...pushy." She held his hand for a moment. "I like nice guys who don't talk much."

He glanced at her hand on his. "He used to be a lot worse before he got married. He can't help it." He shrugged. "It's who he is."

As he put the truck in gear, she saw him smile a little. If she had to guess, Parker had lost a lot of girlfriends to his older brother. Good thing Lucas had been taken off the market.

Chapter Eight

"Renee's grandmother doesn't like me," Lucas said at breakfast the next morning.

Parker grabbed another English muffin off the plate in the middle of the table. "She likes me and Miss Dee. What did you do to get on her bad side?"

"Nothing. I talked to Renee, nice and polite. I minded all the manners Mom beat into me." He paused. "At least, I thought I did. Why doesn't she like me?"

Parker grinned. "She thinks you're pushy."

"You're enjoying this, aren't you?"

"Oh, yeah. It's nice to know the great ladies' man, Lucas Callahan, has lost some of that charm he used to use on every woman he met. Marriage agrees with you more and more every day. I approve."

They ate in silence for a few minutes before Lucas looked up. "Did you tell Renee you can see ghosts yet? Or that you're a spiritual conduit to help said ghosts cross over?"

"No. I don't want her to think I'm weird." Parker refilled his glass. "I saw her grandmother when they first arrived at the B and B. Miss Dee offered my services to help her look for the oak tree where her grandparents got engaged."

"She said you were helping her with a small task. Searching all those trees isn't a small task by any stretch of the imagination." He spread strawberry jam on an English muffin. "You can't do the crossing over ritual until Halloween and that's a week and a half away." Lucas glanced at him. "Her grandmother will go to the other side then."

"I know." Parker stood and picked up their empty plates and carried them to the sink. "I'm going to have to tell her she can't spread the ashes until Halloween. Then, I'm going to have to explain why. I hope she understands."

"I believe she'll understand more than you think." Lucas leaned back in his chair and watched his brother wash their few dishes. "As Green Men, we each have unique abilities. We're two sides of the same coin, death and birth. We both help the souls of those living and dead. Me with my flowers and you with the help you give to ghosts. I believe Renee can not only see her grandmother, she also has the talent to see other ghosts. You two might be made for each other."

Parker looked at him over his shoulder. "Did you pick up the gift of divination recently and not tell me?"

"No, but I saw her try not to laugh when I felt her grandmother's spirit go through me." Lucas finished his orange juice and handed his glass to Parker to wash out. "You have more in common with her than anyone, and that includes me. My talent lies with life and growth."

"And with the new wife."

"You got that right, and that's one talent I enjoy." Lucas smiled and left the room.

Parker walked out to his truck and sat in it for a few minutes. His brother made a lot of sense. He smiled. Two sides of the same coin. He'd never thought of them that way. He started the truck and headed to the bed and breakfast. Telling Renee about what he could do no longer seemed to worry him. Now, it gleamed as bright as a ray of sunshine.

****

"Have you noticed how handsome most of the men are in this town?" Gran said. "Even that man, Mac, who runs the general store. He's rather attractive for an older gent. It's like someone bottled up all the cuteness and dumped it here. I wish were alive to appreciate them more."

Renee pulled the pillow over her head. "I don't need to hear this right now. Are you sure you don't need to rest or sleep or dematerialize to conserve energy? Your observations are getting a little on the risqué side." She gave in and sat up, leaning back against the headboard. "Why don't you like Parker's brother?"

"He's a bit mouthy for my tastes. Good looks only go so far with me. I can't believe how he flirted with you." Gran folded her arms and frowned. "Made me happy when you put him in his place. He's not like Parker at all."

"You, of all people, or ghosts as the case may be, know all siblings are different." She stretched and swung her legs over the side of the bed. "I think Lucas is okay, if a little full of himself. Parker said he can't help it, and he acted worse before he got married. You can tell the two of them are related. They look a lot alike."

Renee got up to do her usual routine. She skipped the shower. It felt pointless to get all cleaned up and then go hike in the woods. She thought again about the heaviness in the north side woods. Part of her wanted to explore deeper, but another part wanted to avoid the whole area.

"Gran, did you find out any more information about the woman in the woods?" She tied her boots. "You were with me when I found out from Sara Callahan that her name is Lily McGee. Did any ghost tell you why she hasn't crossed over yet?"

Gran stared out the window. "She doesn't want to leave. Her child is still missing. She wants to cross over, but she can't. Not until she knows the truth."

"I wish the historical society had more information. Sara Callahan told us what she knew, but it was more speculation than anything." She grabbed her sweater. "I wonder if anyone knows the truth or if the rumors have grown because no one knows what really happened."

"I'm sorry, my dear. I wish I had the answers you want, but I hadn't even heard of Lily's story when I met your grandfather here. Of course, it could have happened after we moved back east."

"It's okay, Gran. I'm sure we'll find out before I have to leave."

Renee walked down to breakfast, her thoughts more jumbled than a jigsaw puzzle. She came here for one simple task. All she had to do was spread her grandmother's ashes, then go home. Now, she found herself hip deep in a mystery she hadn't expected. She couldn't leave the poor soul out there forever. Determination filled her to find out what had happened.

Somehow, she had to find the answers Lily McGee deserved. She headed straight for the buffet trays and loaded a plate. She sat in her usual spot as Dee walked in from the kitchen.

"Hi, Miss Dee."

"Good morning, Renee." She set a tray of her usual

warm cinnamon rolls in the center of the table. "My, you look like you have your mind set on a serious task today."

She took a bite of her breakfast. "I do. What can you tell me about the tragedy in the north woods?"

Dee sat silent for a moment or two. "Lily McGee ran from her husband, and he caught her in the woods. She tried to keep her son from him, but he took the baby."

A baby boy. Another piece to the puzzle. "Do you have any idea what happened to him?"

"No one does. The town never found the child. There are lots of rumors, but the favorite is, the fairies took the baby. That's the one everyone wants to have happened. I guess we'll never know."

Renee propped her head up on her hand. Good thing she wasn't a detective. These dead ends were making her crazy. She faced frustration after mounting frustration. She wouldn't even know how to begin to get adoption records. The baby had to be the key to this whole scenario.

Dee stood and smiled. "Why don't you ask the fairies? No one ever has, but I think they may tell you what happened that night."

"You aren't serious, are you?"

"Very serious. There's magic around you all the time." She nodded and smiled at someone over Renee's shoulder. "There's even ghosts and some besides Lily who may need your help."

"Miss Dee," Renee said. "Can you see my grandmother?"

Dee smiled and took the dirty dishes to the kitchen.

Okay. Garland Falls got weirder all the time. Renee

glanced at her grandmother's ghost and Gran shrugged. This time when they went to the woods, Renee would look for signs of a fairy ring. She used to read about fairies all the time growing up, so she knew what fairy rings looked like. She huffed out a breath and wished for the knowledge on how to talk to fairies. The front door opened, and she jerked upright when Parker walked in.

"You ready to tackle more of the north woods today?" he asked.

"Sure. Let me grab my jacket."

How could the man brighten a whole room and her mood just by coming inside? Oh, who cared? As long as he kept doing it.

They headed toward the woods, and Renee shivered before she zipped her jacket up all the way. "I didn't realize the wind would be so brisk today. I should've brought a hat. My ears are going to be raw by the time we get back."

He pulled a knit beanie out of his coat pocket. "Minnesota isn't for the unprepared. It gets colder here sooner than the other states. When the fall and winter winds come, it blows right through you."

She pulled the hat over her hair. "Thanks. I guess I need to go into town again and get a few more supplies. At this rate, I think I'll be here longer than I thought."

Somehow, it didn't feel like the worst scenario anymore. She glanced at Parker, sure he was the reason for her change in attitude. Maybe Gran had been right the whole time with all of her matchmaking. If so, being matched with Parker Callahan had to be Gran's best one yet.

Chapter Nine

Renee took a deep breath as they started on a narrow path into the north woods. The oppressive air replaced the usual crisp scents of autumn. Even the sunshine felt heavy on her shoulders. She dashed a tear from the corner of her eye, afraid if she started to weep, she'd never stop. She tried to force those emotions down, but it got harder the deeper they went into this part of the woods. Gran's presence gave her some comfort, but for the first time, it wasn't enough.

"While we look for the tree, can we also keep an eye out for a fairy ring?" she asked, forcing lightness into her voice.

Parker halted. His back went stiff, and his shoulders tightened. "What? Why do you want to look for a fairy ring?"

"Miss Dee told me to ask the fairies about the tragedy here." She gave him a brief smile. "After all, it can't hurt."

"You don't know what you're asking. Forest fairies are flighty and may not want to talk to you. Worse, they could try to lead you deeper into the woods to get you lost."

"Hold up a second." Renee stepped in front of him. "I wasn't serious, but you sound like you think fairies are real."

"These woods are old. Like centuries old. No one

knows for sure if fairies are real or not, or even if they live here at all."

Renee leaned closer to him. "But you think they're here and that they are very real, don't you?"

Parker walked around her and stopped by a large maple tree. He laid his hand on the trunk and bowed his head. "There are things you don't know about me, about Garland Falls. We'd better find your oak tree. The sooner we do, the sooner you can get back to your city life and your boyfriend."

Did he stumble on the word boyfriend? "We don't have to look for fairy rings if you don't want. Let's get back to our search for the oak tree." She smiled. "I find I'm not in too much of a hurry to leave Garland Falls. It's starting to grow on me."

"What about your boyfriend?"

She shrugged. "What about him? I've thought about ending it with him for the past couple of months. I feel like we're going through the motions of a relationship. There's no real emotion between us anymore. I don't think there ever has been."

Parker turned and stared at her. As she watched, he stumbled forward into her arms. She saw the sea captain's ghost as he floated by the tree. He saluted before he disappeared, and she turned her attention to the man she held close. She should let him go, like right now. As she held him, butterflies danced along her spine and twirled in her stomach. Her arms broke out in goosebumps. Warmth spread through her body, letting itself cuddle against her heart.

Could this be what love felt like? If so, she could get used to feeling like this all the time.

****

Parker tried to be angry at the captain but couldn't. The ghost had forced him to take the step he'd been too afraid to. Renee looked so beautiful when the speckled sunlight highlighted her hair. Her green eyes had sparkled when she talked about the fairy ring. Of course, he knew the location of the fairy ring. He would hold the ritual there when the new moon rose on Halloween.

He held her close, and she fit against him like she had been made for him. He'd never wanted someone as much as Renee Tate. Her warm, soft skin smelled like fresh flowers on a crisp autumn day. How could he let her go after she accomplished her goal? He hadn't wanted to get close to her to avoid heartbreak when she left. Well, he'd failed that plan. She wormed her way under his skin and into his heart from the moment he first laid eyes on her.

The moment had come to tell her about himself. Yet he couldn't bring himself to do it. "If you want to look for fairy rings, I'll help you. Not sure if you'll get an answer. We should get back to our search for the oak tree first."

He watched as she nodded her head. "Yeah. I guess we should."

Neither of them made a move to break apart. The captain nudged him, a small reminder he still had a task to accomplish. He gave her a light squeeze, then stepped away. A nervous laugh escaped her, and he looked everywhere but at her. He took a step and felt the warmth of her hand in his. He glanced at her, and she smiled.

"Why don't you tell me more about Garland Falls?" She squeezed his hand. "You said there were things I didn't know about the town and about you."

He knew she waited for an answer. Why couldn't he get the words out? "It's just talk. People say you need to have some magic in you to even find the town."

"Well, that's ridiculous. I found it with my GPS. It popped right up." A sly grin curled her lips. "Unless you're saying I have a magic GPS."

"I don't think there are such things as magic GPS's." He shook his head. "Like I said, it's just talk."

They searched in silence for a few minutes. Parker could hear Renee's grandmother saying no to every oak tree they found. Nervousness tied his stomach in knots. What if she meant the tree at the ritual site? Her grandmother and the captain chatted like they were old friends. Why couldn't he be at ease like that in Renee's presence? If he'd learn to talk to more people, like Lucas suggested on numerous occasions, he'd have been able to speak up.

She slowed to a stop, and he halted with her. "What's wrong?" he asked.

"Can't you feel it?" She turned her face upward and closed her eyes. "Lily's here. She's watching us. Her grief is overwhelming."

"You can sense her?"

She nodded. "Can't you?"

Parker gazed between the trees and hoped this time Lily would show herself. He let go of Renee's hand and walked to a large maple tree. "Lily? Are you here? Tell me how to help you."

Heart wrenching sobs echoed around them, bouncing off trees, bushes, and fallen logs. Renee moved up to stand with him. She held onto his arm and looked around.

"Can you see her?" she whispered.

"No. She never shows herself. I can't help her if I can't find her."

The sobs faded away and Renee stared at him. "You can communicate with ghosts, can't you?"

"No," he stammered. "I've done research on how to help spirits cross over. Let's go. I have work to do this afternoon."

They walked around for about another hour with no luck. They returned to the B and B, and he stood in the driveway while she walked to the door. He shifted from foot to foot and cursed himself. He should've come clean when the perfect opportunity presented itself.

"Did you want to come in for lunch?" she asked.

"No, thanks. I've got plants to pick up, and I have to check in with Mrs. Hall. She might need some other items delivered for the fall festival."

"Will I see you for dinner?"

He gave her a small smile. "Sure. That'd be great. Around six again?"

"Sounds good." She laid her hand on the doorknob. "See you later."

****

As soon as she shut the door, she almost skipped to her room. She had another date with Parker Callahan. "Gran, is it possible to fall in love in record time?"

Her grandmother's ghost appeared. "Of course. It happened for me and your grandpa. It also happened for your parents. Why shouldn't it happen for you? I get the feeling you won't need me matchmaking for you any longer. You seem to have found the perfect man yourself."

"If it runs in the family, I guess it should happen for me, too. I love being with Parker. I get a sense we're alike in more ways than one. Do you think he might love me, too?"

"I believe it with every fiber of my ghostly self. From the way he looks at you, I don't think he wants you to leave Garland Falls."

Renee walked to the window and looked out. The autumn leaves drifted to the ground. In another month or two, snow would fall in the same way. How pretty Garland Falls would be covered in sparkly, white snow. It would look like one of those fancy Christmas cards. This little, out of the way town had begun to feel like home.

"I've thought about that a lot. I'm not sure I want to leave. Since I have my own shop, I'd like to see if there's a store for rent. I think the people here would like to have a custom-made leather goods. I haven't seen another one on Main Street." She turned and smiled at her grandmother's ghost. "Do you think I should? I mean, I'd have to talk to the town council and get all the permits and my license to sell. It helps you left me a very tidy sum of money."

"Garland Falls would be lucky to have you," her grandmother said. "It wouldn't hurt to check out the possibility. You should do it. It would be good for you to get out of the city and live somewhere nice."

"You don't fool me for one second, Gran." She frowned. "You also like the idea of me being away from Wayne."

"You caught me. He has a strange quality that makes me nervous when he's around."

Renee turned back to the window. "You never

liked him, did you?"

"I didn't like his attitude, and I never thought he treated you right."

Renee considered her grandmother's words. Wayne wasn't bad or mean to her, but he wasn't very attentive. Most times, he had to be reminded she stood with him in the same room. At company functions or even friends' parties, he tended to ignore her and talk to everyone else. She sighed. That included other men's dates. He just didn't seem like the one for her any longer. A lot of her close friends had told her time and time again to dump him.

Maybe now, she would. Maybe now, she'd realized what all her friends had said for the past two months. Maybe she and Wayne were destined for other people. Her cell phone chimed and pulled her back to the here and now.

"Hello?"

"Hi, baby. Do you miss me yet?"

"Wayne? Um no, I mean yes."

He'd called her and she had no desire to talk to him.

Chapter Ten

"Every time I talk to you, I have to remind you not to call me baby. I don't like it," she said. "I never did, and I never will."

"Hey, sorry," he said, and didn't sound at all contrite. "I wondered if you knew when you'll be home. The company has a big charity function next week and I want my girl on my arm."

She tried to keep her sigh in and barely succeeded. "I won't be back until after Halloween. It's taking longer than I thought to find Gran's special tree."

There was a long pause on his end. "I see."

She knew that tone in his voice. The pitch always dropped an octave when he got annoyed. "I'm sorry. You'll have to go by yourself or maybe you can ask one of the women you spent the whole time with at the last event."

"I told you, they were important clients."

Renee began to pace. "I know what you said, and I know what I saw. Wayne, you may as well know, I think I might move to Garland Falls."

"You can't. I forbid you to make such a rash decision."

She narrowed her eyes, even though he couldn't see. "You…forbid? That's it. We're done. Don't call me anymore. I'll have someone come over and pack up my stuff."

"I'm sorry, sweetheart, really I am. Why don't I come out there and we'll talk."

"Why don't you stay there and realize we were over a long time ago." She sat on the window seat. "I'm sorry, Wayne, but I think this is best for both of us."

She hung up and leaned back. "Well, I did it, Gran. Wayne and I are through."

Her grandmother materialized next to her. "I heard. Are you okay?"

"Better than okay. Now that it's done, I feel great." She got up and laid out clothes on the bed. "And I have a date with Parker for dinner." She grinned. "Now him, I like."

"I'll let you get ready. I want to see if Lily's ghost will come out and talk to me. Have a good time, dear."

Her grandmother vanished and Renee headed for the shower. After the heartbreak of losing her parents and her grandparents, the light at the end of the tunnel of grief no longer felt like a train headed straight for her. Now, warm, cheery sunshine glowed bright instead, and it was all because of a man named Parker Callahan.

****

Parker walked up and down the rows of mums behind his brother's shop. He needed the right color combination for the B and B's front porch. He'd finished the gardens around the foundation several days before. Now the steps and the porch needed a few last touches to be perfect.

He knelt to tag another large mum with dark maroon flowers. A match to it sat right across the row. As he tagged its mate, his brother walked up and pulled a flat cart stacked with ten large containers filled with purple asters and a small shovel.

"You and Renee Tate find her special tree yet?"

Parker glanced over his shoulder. "We've looked every day but haven't had any luck so far."

Lucas squatted down beside him. "Mrs. Hall says you've been kind of scarce this year."

"I've been busy." He continued to check over the mums around him. "I always have a lot to do this time of year, but now Miss Dee wants me to help Renee, too."

"Parker, stop messing with those flowers for a minute and look at me." He waited until he had his brother's attention. Lucas stared at him, then nodded. "Yep. You've got it bad."

"What? The pox?"

"No, you idiot. You're in love. It's one of my talents." He dusted his hands on his pants. "And I went through it myself a couple of months ago, remember? So, I know what I'm talking about."

"Yeah, I remember." Parker stared at the tags in his hands. "I didn't think I'd ever find someone to love me. Even the residents in town avoid me."

Lucas laughed. "No, they don't. You avoid them. The people here love you. They know what your talents are, and trust me, they're okay with them. I tell you all the time to talk to people more. I mean, Mrs. Hall and Miss Dee think the world of you."

"I talk to Renee. She likes me."

Lucas grinned. "Does she like you or love you?"

Parker walked over to two large orange mums and tagged them. "I don't know. I think she might love me. The captain shoved me into her arms, and she held me. She also held my hand today."

"Then, little bro, you need to let her know how you feel."

"Can you get these dug up for me? I also need two light purple and two yellow, all about the same size. I have to go." He grinned at Lucas. "I have a date."

"I don't believe it. You don't date."

He shrugged. "I guess I do now."

Parker got in his truck and drove home. A quick shower and a check of his pockets to make sure he had all he needed. Plenty of cash in his wallet for dinner and whatever else she might want. Maybe he would tell her tonight about himself and what he could do. If his luck held, she'd understand and wouldn't run in the other direction. Lucas believed she had the same abilities as he did. Well, it was time for him to find out for sure.

The truck idled to a stop in the B and B's driveway. Parker walked up to the door and commanded his stomach to settle down. He ran a hand through his hair and straightened his shoulders. The door opened, and Miss Dee stood there and smiled at him.

"Parker Callahan, are you going to come in or stand on the porch all night?"

"I'm coming in. Renee and I have a dinner date."

Miss Dee swung the door open wider. "Oh, I know. Her grandmother told me." She shut the door behind him, and they walked to the drawing room. "She's still upstairs. Have you seen the captain tonight?"

"Not yet. I expect he'll turn up when he's ready." He grinned. "He likes to mess with me."

Miss Dee gestured for him to sit in the wingback chair across from the small couch and stood in front of him. "You've got a lot of nervous energy in you tonight. What's wrong?"

Parker sat and laced and unlaced his fingers. "I like Renee."

"It was obvious to me when you two first met. What else is on your mind?"

"Miss Dee, do you think she'd understand about what I can do?"

She chuckled and kissed the top of his head. "She might be a little shocked at first, but the two of you have almost the same, I guess powers is an appropriate term. I'm not sure if she's a spirit conduit like you, but I bet she has some abilities similar to yours."

"What if I'm wrong?"

Dee waved her hand in the air. "Pish tosh. That girl has already fallen for you, and that's half the battle right there. You tell her whatever she wants to know. You'll see. She'll understand."

He heard footsteps on the stairs. "I hope you're right, Miss Dee," he mumbled.

Renee smiled at him as she entered the drawing room. "Have you been here long? I didn't mean to make you wait."

Parker jumped to his feet. "I've just been here for a few minutes. Should we go?"

"You two have a nice time," Dee said as she headed to the kitchen.

He looked Renee over, and his heart skipped a beat. She had applied light makeup, which made her green eyes stand out. The pale blue shirt accented the fairness of her skin and the auburn highlights in her hair. Black slacks showed off her slim figure and, for a change, her shoes had low heels.

"You look nice," he stammered out.

Her cheeks turned pink under her makeup. "Thanks. So do you."

Wow, he gave her credit for being a good liar. He'd thrown on a pair of black jeans and a faded green, button-down shirt. He wore his work boots, because he had no good shoes. Next to her, he felt shabby and underdressed. He held the door for her, and they walked out to his truck.

Since the diner had more of a date vibe than the pizzeria, they ended up there again. For the first time, Parker wished they had someplace a little fancier in Garland Falls. They sat at the same booth at the back they always seemed to occupy. Sally came and took their orders and hurried off again at her usual breakneck pace.

"So, um, how did the rest of your day go?" he asked.

"Fine. My boyfriend called me, and I broke up with him. I can't believe I stayed with him for so long." She smiled her thanks at Sally when their food appeared as if by magic. "I think I might move to Garland Falls."

Would it be bad manners to dance on the tables at her news? Probably. He took a deep breath and hoped he could play it cool. "That's great. Garland Falls is a nice town."

She glanced up at him. "I'd hoped you'd like the idea. I still have to think about it some more, but my mind is almost made up. I like it here." She laid her hand over his. "I like the people, too. Some more than others."

He curled his fingers around hers. "I like you, too." He gazed at her for a few minutes when a voice caught his attention. Not Lucas. Not now. "I think my brother's here."

"He waved at the back of your head, so I'd have to say, you're right. Here he comes."

Lucas strode down the aisle and pushed into the booth next to Parker. "Hey, guys. Fancy meeting you here."

Parker smacked his brother's hand when he reached for a French fry. "Not that much of a coincidence. Why are you here?"

"I wanted to make sure you made it to your date." He smiled at Renee. "Nice to see you again. He doesn't date much. I always have to check up on his manners. You know, to make sure he's behaving himself."

Parker shoved his side into his brother and forced Lucas to the edge of the seat. "It's fine. Go home."

"I'm waiting for a to-go order. Thought I'd come over and say hi."

"Hi and goodbye. This is a two-person date." Parker elbowed his in the ribs. "Beat it, before I tell your wife what an obnoxious jerk you're being right now."

Renee coughed and held a napkin in front of her mouth. The way her eyes sparkled, he knew she tried hard not to laugh. She cleared her throat and said, "It's nice to see you again, Lucas, but Parker's right. You need to wait for your order elsewhere."

Lucas gave a dramatic sigh and stood. "I know when I'm not wanted. See you later, little bro."

After he left, Renee said, "Why does Lucas wear a cowboy hat? I mean, Minnesota is nothing like Texas."

Parker glanced over his shoulder at his brother. "He works outside all day. He says it helps to keep his neck from getting burned. My opinion is, he likes to wear it."

Renee laughed. "I think you hit the nail on the head."

Chapter Eleven

Parker and Renee walked to the small park behind the town hall. He waited until she sat at one of the picnic tables before he sat across from her. She loved his manners, his reticence, in fact, everything about him. The real reason for her decision to move here sat across from her, silent and patient. Maybe the time had come for her to tell him she could see and talk to ghosts. Keeping a secret this big was not the best way to start a serious relationship.

She ran her hand across the table to brush away some leaves and dust. "Parker, there's a fact about me you should know, and I don't want you to think I'm some kind of a nut."

"Okay," he said slowly. "I promise to keep an open mind."

As soon as she opened her mouth, her phone buzzed in her pocket. She ignored the vibration until it stopped, and then it started up again. "I'd better take this. It might be important and if I don't, it'll ring the whole time I want to talk to you. Back in a second."

She got up and walked to the next table and sat with her back to Parker. "Wayne, why are you calling me?" she whispered. "I told you we're done."

"I can't believe that," he said. "I know I haven't paid very much attention to you lately. I've put in for a promotion and had to do extra work. It'll mean more money for us."

"You mean, more money for you. If you paid me half the attention you do to your job and other women, we might've been able to work this out." She sighed. "You're a workaholic and a ladies' man, Wayne. You always will be, and I don't blame you for that. It's who you are, but I need more. Please don't call me again."

She hung up, turned her phone off, and walked back over to where Parker waited for her to come back. The expression on his face almost broke her heart. He must have thought she wanted to get back together with Wayne. Time to set him straight about her former relationship.

"Was it important like you thought?" he asked.

"Not even close." She folded her arms and leaned on the table. "Where were we?"

"You didn't want me to think you were some kind of a nut."

She swung her legs over the bench and gazed at him. "Don't you want to know about my phone call?"

"That's your private business."

"It is, but I want you to know. My ex-boyfriend called me. I broke up with him again. I don't think he can take a hint."

Parker smiled and squeezed her hand. "I can take hints. Now tell me why you're nuts."

"I have this weird ability," she said. "Gran always told me it's passed down through her side of the family." She took a deep breath, then blurted out, "I can see and talk to ghosts."

His expression never changed. "Is that why your grandmother hangs around you? Because you can see and talk to her?"

Renee blinked several times, not believing what he'd said. "You can see her, too?"

He walked around the table and sat next to her. "I see ghosts everywhere. I'm not exactly human."

"Then, what are you?" she whispered.

"There's a lot of tales and legends passed down through the centuries about the Green Man. He's a forest spirit. Some beliefs state he's a figure of rebirth and brings new life in the spring. But there's another side to birth and that's death."

She leaned closer to him. "What has all this got to do with you? Why aren't you human?"

"My brother and I are Green Men. We're from the fairy realm. His ability lies in birth and life. He grows all kinds of flowers and plants. He's also the guardian of a special flower that arrives just before the beginning of spring and blooms on the vernal equinox. We think it was his power that made him such a ladies' man most of his life."

"I guess that would explain why he's such a flirt," she said.

He rubbed a hand over his eyes. "My ability is to help the dead cross over. It's a rebirth for the soul. I hold the ritual twice a year. Once during the first new moon of spring and the second on Halloween night."

"Okay." Renee took several minutes to digest what he'd said. He couldn't be crazy. If so, she'd have to join him on the crazy train. "Why Halloween?" she asked. "Why not the first new moon of fall?"

"All those stories about the veil between worlds being thinnest on Halloween are true. With All Saints Day on November first and All Souls Day on November second, the guiding light to the afterlife is brightest then."

She was quiet for a moment. "Makes sense," she finally said. "With what I can do, it doesn't sound as strange as you thought it would. I've got a few questions, if you don't mind." Renee held his hand a little tighter, and his tremors slowed. She ran her thumb over his knuckles. "How do you do it? Cross them over, I mean."

"I'm a conduit for spirits. They find me, and I lead them to the site. I gather specific flowers and lay them in a circle. I draw strength from the earth and open the gateway. That's all there is to it."

"Will you cross over Gran when the time comes?"

He nodded. "If she wants to go. Some ghosts hang around because they like it here. On Halloween, if she agrees, I'll cross her over to the afterlife. We'll find her oak tree, and you can spread her ashes after the ritual."

"What about the sea captain I've seen? Will he go too?"

Parker shrugged. "I ask him every year, and every year he says he's not ready."

They rose and meandered through the small park. "And the ghost of Lily McGee? What about her?"

"She won't talk to me. I can't send her to the other side if I can't find her."

Renee held his hand tighter. "I believe she stays because she misses her child. If we can tell her what happened to the baby, maybe she'll want to cross over then."

Parker cupped her cheek and smiled. "It takes a special woman to hear what I said and not run from me."

"It appears we have almost the same abilities. I

don't think I'm a conduit, though, and I'm pretty sure I'm not from the fairy realm." She pressed his hand to her cheek. "I'm glad I met you, Parker Callahan. It's nice not having to hide what I can do around someone I like."

He leaned closer, and his breath warmed her lips. When he paused, she closed the gap and placed a light kiss on his. He stared at her, and her face burned. Her heart thumped to a wild beat in her chest as goosebumps ran up and down her spine. Sparks ran through her veins, and she wanted to dance. Love should always feel like this. Whatever she had with Wayne, it sure didn't feel like what she had right here, right now with Parker.

"If you want me to apologize, I won't," she said.

He shook his head. "I want to see if I should kiss you again. If you don't mind, I think I will."

The second felt even better than the first time around. He held her so close, his heart beat against her chest in time to her own. Perspiration popped out on her forehead from the heat of his kiss. The feeling of his lips on hers made her body run hot and cold. When he ended the kiss, she laid her head on his shoulder and held him tight. He was warm and strong and could talk to ghosts like her. She'd never leave Garland Falls now.

"I think we have something good here, Parker," she whispered.

"I agree."

They walked through the park a little longer, until the wind began to blow harder. Leaves swirled around their feet. Renee scuffed along the sidewalk and kicked at the small piles nestled against the edge of the lawns. They made their way back to his truck and got in. He started it and turned toward the Bed and Breakfast.

He parked in front of the B and B. "I'll see you tomorrow so we can get back to the search for the oak tree."

"I'll be ready." She gave him another quick kiss. "Good night."

She got out and waved before she went inside. Up in her room, she got ready for bed, Parker never far from her thoughts. He'd been a missing piece in her life, and she never realized it until she met him. She sat on the bed, her thoughts a whirlwind as she considered all the steps she needed to do for the move.

"Did you have a good time tonight?" Gran asked. "It looks like you did. You have a nice rosy glow in your cheeks."

"Parker kissed me tonight. Well actually, I kissed him first, so yes. I had a great time." She hesitated. "Gran, I've decided to move here. Since I own my own shop, I can pick up and go anywhere."

Her grandmother floated next to her on the bed. "Why, that's a fine idea. You should do it."

"There's a lot for me to check into, like if there's a property for rent. Then I have to go get my stuff, close the down the other shop, pay the taxes. There's a lot to do to make this happen." She gazed at her grandmother's ghost. "I'll have to sell your house."

"I know, dear. I don't need it any longer. You do what you need to make your move here. I'm sure you're up to the task."

"I'm sure I am." She grabbed her nightshirt. "You know, Gran? I never thought a man could give me wobbly knees, but Parker can, and I think I like it."

Chapter Twelve

Renee turned off her alarm, stretched, and sat up. "Gran, are you around?"

"I'm always near you, my dear. What do you need?"

Renee got up and laid out her clothes for the day. "Did you get a chance to try to talk to Lily's ghost last night?"

"She doesn't want to be found or to talk to anyone." Gran floated as she paced. "I'd love to find out what happened to her child. That poor woman has suffered for so long."

"Parker and I want to try to find out so we can give her some peace. Unfortunately, I have no idea how to begin."

"You'll figure it out, I'm sure." The ghost followed her into the bathroom. "I knew I liked Parker as soon as I saw him, unlike his pushy brother. He's got a good soul."

"Lucas isn't so bad, and it's not his fault he's a flirt. It's a kind of side effect of his powers. Parker said he got married a couple of months ago. The brothers are supernatural beings called Green Men. I'm going to have him explain more about their origin later." She stood and grabbed her clothes. "Now, if you don't mind, I'd like to shower."

She showered and dressed and stared out the

window while she brushed her hair. Parker's truck was parked outside already. He must be as anxious as she to be together again. She pulled her hair up in a ponytail and hurried downstairs. He'd already helped himself to breakfast. If the pile on his plate indicated anything, the man could pack it away with the best of them. How on earth did he looked so good, eating so much food? Who cared? She could stare at him all day and never lose a second's interest.

"You eat enough to feed an army," she said. "Do all Green Men eat that much?"

"I'll never tell." He smiled. "We've got a lot of ground to cover today. Load up. We might not make it back in time for lunch."

Dee came out of the kitchen with a tray of warm bread. "Well hello, you two. Are you back on the tree hunt today?"

"Yes, we are. I hope we'll have more luck than we've had so far," Renee said. "I wish Gran could've told me the tree's location. This is ridiculous. Every oak tree is wrong, or so she says." Renee stopped and stared at Miss Dee, her eyes opened wide. "I mean…"

Miss Dee patted her shoulder. "I know what you meant. Don't worry. Your secret is safe with me." She winked. "I have quite a few secrets of my own."

They finished up and stepped out into the sunshine. Renee took a deep breath "It's so pretty here."

"Wait until winter hits. You won't think it's so pretty then."

"I bet I will."

She looped her arm through his, and they started off for the north woods again. They continued the search for the elusive oak tree and hoped to catch a glimpse of Lily McGee's ghost.

"I have a special place I want to show you, if you don't mind," Parker said.

"I don't mind, as long as you're with me. What do you want me to see?"

He smiled and took a different path than the usual ones. The trees were denser here, and the underbrush grew thick as they pushed through it. Morning fog still covered the ground where the sun had yet to poke through the thick, leafy canopy. She shivered in the cool shade, the atmosphere affecting her more than the temperature.

The air stilled, and the normal sounds of the woods quieted as well. Her steps slowed and she glanced behind them, wanting more than ever to turn back. Parker held her hand tighter and smiled. The warmth of his hand in hers forced her jumpy nerves settle down.

"Here we are." He moved a wall of vines aside to reveal a clearing. In the center grew an uneven circle of mushrooms. "You wanted to find a fairy ring. There's one in here. Do you still want to talk to the fairies?"

"I'm not sure. I mean, you told me fairies are real. It was different when I thought they were still a fantasy. I don't know if I should talk to them." She shrank back against him. "What if I say the wrong thing? What if I make them mad?"

He chuckled. "Most fairies don't take too much offense. They know how humans can be. We can try to summon them, if you like."

"Not right now. I guess I'm not as brave as I thought."

He kissed her forehead. "You're very brave. Don't ever think you aren't. Come on. Let's get back to our search."

As they left the clearing, Renee looked over her shoulder. A real fairy ring. Maybe one day she'd summon fairies, but not today. Definitely not today.

****

They returned to the B and B around two in the afternoon. Renee's shoulders sagged as, once again, her grandmother's oak tree remained elusive.

Parker pulled her close. "Are you okay? You seem a little down."

"I'm fine. I don't think we'll ever find the tree." She sighed. "I have a sneaky suspicion Gran isn't trying very hard to help us."

"Why?"

She sighed. "Gran is a matchmaker from way back. I don't think being dead would stop her." She brightened. "I'm glad we already like each other."

"Me, too." Parker waved to Dee. "Hey, Miss Dee, we're back. Is there anything else you'd like me to pick up to finish the decorations?"

He paid more attention to Renee than what Miss Dee listed. He nodded and murmured agreement when he should, but Renee Tate occupied all of his thoughts at the moment. Her cheeks were pink from the chilly October air, her hair mussed from the breeze. Her eyes sparkled when she smiled at him and made his heart beat wildly in his chest. He knew magic worked fast when it came to matters of the heart, but this went more quickly than anything he'd heard of before.

"I have to go pick up a few things Miss Dee requested. Want another trip into town?" he asked.

"Sure. There are still stores I need to explore. Let me go put on my other jacket. Be right back."

Parker dropped her off on Main Street and made the same arrangements as before to pick her up. He drove out to Lucas' fields. He hoped his brother had gotten his order together. The mums he'd selected the day before were perfect and he couldn't wait to display them.

"Hey, Parker. Your order's ready. We got the mums potted for you this morning," Lucas said.

Parker looked over the flowers and nodded. "They look good. Must be handy to know when I want them."

"It helps when the plants tell me. I got here as the sun rose to make sure I had your order completed." Lucas paused, then grinned. "How's things with Ms. Tate?"

"As well as can be expected. Before you ask, no. We still haven't found her grandmother's tree yet." He examined the mums. "We finally confessed our abilities to each other. You were right. She wasn't surprised when I told her I could do the same thing she could."

"I told you so. As the older brother, I'm obligated to give you the benefit of my wisdom and experience." Lucas turned serious and lifted his face to the slight breeze. "The woods, the flowers, even the air feels different this year. I can't sense the usual anticipation of rebirth. There's more heaviness now than the last few decades. Do you think it's because of your new lady friend?"

"I don't think it's any coincidence that Renee's here now. The last time we felt this kind of heaviness was when Lily McGee met her end. We were only kids then, and we knew something had gone horribly wrong." Parker also let the breeze caress his face. "I've sensed it, too, around Miss Dee's place. Renee may be the catalyst we need to help Lily's spirit."

"At this point, anything's possible." Lucas looked around and lowered his voice. "Some of the wood sprites told me they've heard whispers of The Hunt returning to the area. They've even said they've heard the hounds baying. If it's true…"

Parker stared at his brother, interrupting him before he could finish. "The Hunt can't return here. Garland Falls has been given more protections after his last appearance. It hasn't been this safe for several decades." His heart began a staccato beat, and his breath came in short bursts. His hands turned cold and clammy, and he wiped them on his jeans. "Have you alerted Mrs. Hall?"

"Yes." Lucas helped him place the flowers on a small cart. "After the close call we had this past spring, she and the town elders have gone out to make sure the wards and runes are reinforced. They go out at least three times a week to be sure there aren't any problems." He leaned on the tailgate. "The Huntsman has always been incredibly powerful. I'm worried our protections may not be enough if we can sense him already. He might get through this year."

"Good point. His power might have grown substantially since his last appearance." Parker loaded the mums in the back of his truck and slammed the tailgate shut. "Whatever happens, this will be the most eventful Halloween we've had in a long time."

****

Renee meandered by the shop windows and checked out the wares for sale. More than ever, she knew her store would be a great addition to Main Street. People smiled and waved. Most called out hellos. This had to be the friendliest town she'd ever been in. If a storefront would come up for rent, she'd take that as a definite sign she should move here.

She stopped in front of the cookie shop. The sign over the door read "Heavenly Bites." She inhaled the delicious aroma wafting out, tasting the buttery cookies without ever having taken a bite. Pumpkins, gourds of all colors, figures of pilgrims, and a large cornucopia filled with all kinds of fruits, vegetables, and fall leaves sat in the window.

"Oh, I have to go in there," she murmured. "Like right now."

Renee stepped inside and inhaled deeply, savoring the scent of vanilla, chocolate, coconut, and a lot of other delicious aromas. A petite woman with short, brown hair stood at the register. She walked up and peered in the case. "This has got to be the most appropriately named store ever. There's so many to choose from. Got any recommendations?"

"Sure." She stared at Renee for a few minutes. "You'd like to have a chocolate swirl, a sugar cookie with rainbow sprinkles, and a hot chocolate."

Renee laughed. "It's like you read my mind."

"It's a gift." She stuck her hand out. "Joanna Mines."

"Renee Tate. How do you stay so thin working here?"

Joanna put the two cookies on a plate and poured the hot chocolate in a mug. "It takes a lot of discipline and I never have time to stand still. There's always work to be done, and the customers keep me on my toes when they come in. Are you visiting someone here in town?"

Renee paid for her food. "No. My grandmother requested in her will I spread her ashes around a certain tree at Warner's Bed and Breakfast."

"Oh, I'm sorry."

"It's okay." She took her order to a table by the window, and Joanna followed her. "I thought once I found the tree, I'd do what she wanted and go back home."

"And now?"

"If I can find a store to rent and a place to live, I want to move here. It's such a wonderful little town."

Joanna laughed. "Garland Falls has a way of getting to a person. I was on my way to Vancouver and, as you can see, I never left."

A tall, slim man with long, white-blond hair came out of the back. "Slacking on the job, Jo?"

"I don't slack, and you know it. I made a new friend. Renee, this is my husband, Davin Mines. Davin, this is Renee Tate. She told me she'll move here if a store comes up for rent before she leaves."

"You'd be a nice addition to the town, Renee. Keep checking. I'm sure you'll find the perfect location."

Joanna jumped to her feet. "Oops. Here comes the afternoon crowd. You take your time, and I'll check on you after I take care of the mob."

Renee ate and sipped the hot chocolate. She liked Joanna and Davin. As she watched Joanna run back and forth, she understood how the woman stayed in shape. She kept up a hectic pace, as she talked and waited on everyone at the same time. At least, that's how it looked to Renee. The whole time, her bright smile never faltered.

When she finished, she stood and waved to the

couple then stepped outside. As she continued her tour of the shops, a For Rent sign appeared in a window that moments before had merchandise in it. Someone or some force appeared to know what she'd said to Joanna. Another definite sign this was the place for her.

Well, Garland Falls had ghosts and a devastatingly handsome man who claimed kinship with fairies. Why couldn't there be a little magic here, also?

Chapter Thirteen

Renee held the phone away from her ear, until Wayne went quiet.

"Now that you're done, I have some news to tell you," she said. "I've made the decision to move to Garland Falls. I'll be back after Halloween to sell Gran's house and pack up my stuff."

He waited another minute. "You can't mean this."

"I'm sorry if this decision hurts you," Renee said. "But you know this is the right move for me. It's also the best move for you. You don't need me around to help you make a good impression on your boss. He already thinks the world of you."

"Yeah, but why Garland Falls? I don't like you out there by yourself. How about if I come out and we'll talk. Maybe we can fix our relationship."

She sighed. "I've been over this with you several times. There's nothing to fix. Our relationship ended at least six months ago. Neither one of us mentioned it because I think we got comfortable with the routine. You have to admit we've just been going through the motions of a relationship. Once you think about it, you'll realize I'm right. I'll be back after Halloween. We'll talk then, okay? Bye."

"But Renee…"

"Bye, Wayne."

She shut off her phone and sat on the bed. "Gran,

why do you think Wayne hates this town so much when he's never been here? He's so against me moving here. I can't understand his attitude."

Gran floated back and forth in an imitation of pacing. "Maybe Wayne has more secrets than you realize."

"Thanks for not mentioning how I've kept my own secret about talking to ghosts from him." Renee fell back on her bed. "It figures he'd have his own secrets to keep, too. Of course, I shouldn't be surprised. Everyone has secrets, whether they know it or not. I wish he'd realize we're done. I've told him not to call me anymore." She pushed up and walked to the window. "I have to let Parker know I need to go back for about a week. I hope he doesn't worry I want back with Wayne, because that won't ever happen."

Gran floated next to her. "I don't think Parker will worry too much. I'm pretty sure he knows how infatuated with him you are. Maybe he'll go with you to help you pack."

Renee smiled. "He'd be great to have along, but he already told me he doesn't like cities. He'll stay here and I'll be gone a week, two at most."

She stared at the calendar on the wall. "Halloween will be here before we know it. Gran, you have to help me find that tree. As much as I don't want to lose you, I want you to have the peace you deserve. Don't you think Gramps has waited for you long enough?"

"I suppose you're right. I'll try harder to remember where it's located, Renee. Sometimes, I don't want to leave you, either." She placed her fingers on Renee's cheek, making her shiver. "I miss my old man, and I'm looking forward to seeing him again."

Renee sniffed, then glanced at the clock. "I've got to get a move on. Parker and I are going out on another hunt for your oak tree." She stared at the shirt in her hands. "I wish there was more information about Lily's child."

"Even Sara at the Historical Society couldn't tell you that," Gran said. "Now hop to it. I've told you before, never let a handsome man wait on you."

Renee rushed through her routine and hurried down the stairs. Parker's voice reached her as he discussed the decorations with Dee. Even his voice sent tremors of excitement through her. She had the big "It" bad, the "It" being love. She never thought she'd have someone so wonderful like Parker Callahan in her life.

"Good morning," she said, as she stepped into the foyer.

"Hi," Parker said. "You look like you're ready to go out on another serious search."

She snapped out a salute. "Ready when you are, captain."

Dee chuckled and adjusted two yellow mums on either side of the door. "You haven't eaten yet. Would you like to take a small snack with you?"

"Do you mean your delicious cinnamon rolls?" Renee sniffed the air. "Because I can smell them and I'd never say no to those."

"I do indeed."

Renee sighed. "Awesome. Can I have two?"

Parker straightened up. "Excuse me, how about four? You have to feed your guide, too, you know."

Dee laughed and went to get the rolls. She handed them a blue vinyl lunch bag and shooed them out the door. As soon as her feet hit the driveway, Renee pulled out one of the rolls and devoured it. When Parker stared at her, she shrugged.

"Maybe I should've had breakfast before we started," she said.

Parker took her hand. "I tell you what. We'll make it a short search today and I'll buy you a big lunch."

"Deal."

They walked into the woods on the north side of the bed and breakfast. He led them down yet another trail, and her grandmother said no at every tree. "Can we go back to the fairy ring? Maybe the tree is there," she said. "We didn't search too much in that area."

"It's almost lunchtime. How about if we start over there tomorrow?"

"Okay." Did he avoid going back to the clearing? Well, fine with her, for now. "If you think that's best, but I want to check out the clearing when we have more time."

They walked across the lawn, and Renee's shoulders sagged in relief to see the B and B. Her stomach growled, and she knew should've eaten more. The cinnamon rolls were huge and delicious but couldn't take the place of a real breakfast. They got in Parker's truck and soon found themselves back at the diner. She didn't mind. She liked the good food and the comfortable atmosphere.

She ordered a big lunch and when Sally set it down, she worried maybe she ordered too much. Parker smiled as she dug in. After she took her first bite of the sandwich, she knew she ordered just the right amount. The sandwich almost melted in her mouth and there wouldn't be any problems with finishing it. Parker's plate held twice as much as hers and he was more than halfway done.

She wiped her mouth and sat back. "Who do I talk to about leasing a commercial property?"

"There should be a contact number on the sign. Then you go to the clerk's office and get your permit to sell and your license and that should be it. Did you find a place already?"

Parker paid the check, and Renee took his hand when they walked outside. "Yes, I did. Something strange happened. I had taken a quick break in Heavenly Bites and started talking to Joanna, you know her, right?" When he nodded, she continued. "I told her I'd move here if I could find a store to rent. I'm in business for myself and when I went outside, a store had come available. I could've sworn that store had been occupied when I went into Heavenly Bites. I felt like it waited for me to find it."

"Sounds about right. A lot of the people who live here believe the town has a mind of its own. No one knows how Garland Falls decides who it likes and who it doesn't."

She walked in front of him and stopped. "Parker, tell me the truth. Is anything about Garland Falls or its people normal?"

He took a deep breath. "No. Not in the least."

She stood silent for a moment, then shrugged. "Okay. Let me see about how to get my store."

"Wait, just like that, you're okay with the strangeness here?"

"Oh, please." She waved her hand in a nonchalant manner. "I communicate with the dead. I think I fit right in."

"True." He grinned at her. "Would you like to meet

Mrs. Hall? She organizes all the town's events and festivals."

"Sure."

Parker took her to the town hall. Shouts, laughter, and the staccato banging of hammers drifted out of the open doors they walked toward. Renee looked around in amazement. Preparations for the Halloween festival were in full swing. If an open spot could be found on any wall, it didn't stay empty for long. Pumpkins and hay bales sat in piles on the floor. Ghosts and bats floated on strings from the ceiling. Black cats and witches covered the walls. In between everything were red, orange, brown, and gold leaves. Signs had been taped to the walls, signifying what tables were placed where. In the middle of the chaos stood a short, stout woman with gray hair, a friendly smile, and a commanding attitude. She looked like a general with her own private army of decorators.

"Mrs. Hall." Parker had to shout to be heard over the workers. When she approached, he smiled. "I'd like you to meet Renee Tate. She wants to open her own shop on Main Street. Renee, this is Mrs. Hall."

Renee shook the woman's hand and grinned. "It's such a pleasure to meet you, Mrs. Hall. I hope after I move here, I can help you with some of the events."

"Welcome to Garland Falls, Renee." She tapped her chin. "Tate. Tate. I knew your grandparents, Esther and Arthur. I heard of their passing. Please accept my condolences. I liked them very much."

"Thank you." Renee glanced around the hall, giving the lump in her throat time to go down. "The decorations look wonderful. This town must enjoy Halloween a lot."

"Garland Falls likes all the holidays," Mrs. Hall said. "We have a Christmas carnival, a spring festival, and so many in the summer, I don't have time to list them all. We have a healthy belief in community, and events bring people together."

Renee was almost bouncing on her toes. "I can't wait to be a part of it all."

"And we can't wait to have you here. Parker, you'd best get this girl home." She grinned. "Then, I have more errands for you to run."

"I had a feeling you'd say that," he said.

They drove by the empty store and Renee wrote down the contact phone number. After Parker dropped her off, she'd take the first step and call to get the information about rent, taxes, and all the paperwork she needed to run a business in this close-knit community.

Parker pulled up to the front door of the B and B. Renee got out and stopped dead in her tracks. Wayne sat in one of the rockers. He ran down the steps and pulled her into his arms, kissing her cheek.

"Hello, sweetheart. I missed you so much."

Chapter Fourteen

Parker watched as Renee pushed out of Wayne's arms. This was the guy she'd been dating in her back east city? He looked too soft, too urban, and too self-absorbed. He'd bet the light brown color in Wayne's hair had been created in a salon, not by being outside in the sunshine. It looked like the only work this man did was on a computer, and that he went to the gym when he felt like it. Wayne could never do his groundskeeper job, with all the hard work he put in day after day.

"Wayne, why the heck are you here?" Renee said. "I told you we were done, over, through."

"And I know you don't mean it." Wayne tried to take her hands, and Parker smiled when she evaded his grasp. "Since I couldn't convince you over the phone to come home, I decided to try in person. I'm not sure what hold this one-horse town has over you, but I know you can't live without the city."

Renee backed away and grabbed Parker's arm. "This man is why I want to stay. He understands me. He doesn't look at other women or talk to them when we're together. I don't play second banana to his job. I'm sick of the city, Wayne. I'm tired of being pushed to the background by you every time we're in public. Parker is the man for me. You need to find a woman who understands you and has the same goals as you."

"You used to have the same goals as me. All you

talked about was making your store more successful."

"I've realized there's more to life than making a ton of money. I like this town and the people are friendly. Being here has opened my eyes to how cold and impersonal city life has become. Our goals these days are vastly different. You need the city and I no longer do. I need the warmth and neighborliness of a small town."

Parker frowned when Wayne eyed him. "Maybe you should go home, Wayne. Renee has decided to move here."

Wayne scowled, then turned to Renee. "Can we go someplace and talk in private?"

"Fine."

Parker grinned as she led him away from the house and down the driveway. He glanced at the sea captain floating off to his left. "I didn't think she'd want him in the gazebo out back. Keep an eye on them for me."

The captain dissipated, and Parker knew he'd stop any shenanigans Wayne might have in mind.

****

Renee lifted a hand to her mouth to hide her smile when the sea captain shoved Wayne and made him stumble. "We have nothing to discuss, Wayne. I don't know why you bothered to come all the way out here. I've made up my mind to move to this town. There's nothing you can say or do to change it. I like Garland Falls. I like the people. For the first time in a long time, I found a place where I'm comfortable and the people are interested in me."

Wayne paced and didn't look at her until he stopped. "You asked me before you left why I didn't want you coming here. Well, here's the real reason. My parents used to live in Garland Falls. People in this town didn't like my father. The people blamed him for every bad situation that happened. It was never his fault, but it didn't seem to matter to them. They said he had a bad temper, but I never saw it. I do know he'd never hurt anyone, especially me or my mother."

Renee's stomach churned as Wayne talked, and bile rose in her throat. Could he be Lily McGee's missing child? "Spit it out. What are you trying to tell me?"

"This town is wrong. I mean really wrong. My father told me my mother died here under strange circumstances. Everyone in town blamed him and didn't believe a strange figure was after him. He took me and we fled to the city where I grew up. Dad passed away my last year of college. His mind began to wander, and he talked about being hunted. He had nightmares that his spirit was in danger. He warned me to never come back here, but I had to." He shook her shoulders. "This is what I want to save you from."

"Are you serious?" She threw his hands off and stepped back. "Dementia is a terrible thing, but it happens to people. It's not caused by an association with a certain town. I don't want to leave here, but if you want to, then go. On second thought, why don't you stay for a few days? It's almost Halloween. I have to go back to close my store and pack my stuff. You're welcome to go back with me." She walked by him, then turned. "And no one is hunting me, except maybe you."

Wayne turned on his heel and stomped away, heading back to the B and B. She walked slowly behind him, and the sea captain appeared next to her. "The young man has said some very troubling things, lass.

Don't be so quick to brush off his concerns."

"I don't understand, captain. What's wrong?"

He faded as he whispered, "Ask Parker about The Hunt."

Renee plodded up the driveway, pondering what the captain had told her. What was The Hunt? Wayne had looked shaken when he mentioned his father's nightmares. Who would want to hunt an old man? When she made it back to the house, Parker still stood by his truck. She walked over and leaned against the fender.

After several long, quiet minutes, she turned to him. "Tell me about The Hunt."

"How did you hear about The Hunt?"

She nodded toward the B and B. "Wayne said his father feared someone had been hunting him and it gave him nightmares. The captain told me to ask you about The Hunt. So, spill. What is it?"

"Let's go to the gazebo."

When he had her settled, he sat next to her. "The Hunt comes around every few decades. The Huntsman is always after prey he can never catch or has his hounds help capture spirits who eluded him before. Garland Falls is supposed to be protected from The Huntsman and his hounds, but they've broken through in the past. The town elders have tried to add better protection spells around the Garland Falls, but he always seems to find the one weak spot and get through."

"Could The Huntsman be the one who killed Lily McGee?"

He shrugged. "It's possible, but the evidence pointed to her husband. Why do you ask?"

"Because there's a strong possibility Wayne is Lily's missing child."

****

Parker didn't expect her to say that, not by a long shot. As he listened to what Renee said about her conversation with Wayne, he had to admit the possibility of her conclusions. Of course, Garland Falls had a tendency to make the impossible possible. His cell phone buzzed in his pocket, and he took it out.

"Hi, Mrs. Hall. What do you need me to do?" He nodded and agreed with whatever she said. He snapped the phone shut and glanced at Renee. "Mrs. Hall said she sensed a new guest. I think she means Wayne. She wants us to bring him to the Halloween festival."

Renee stared at him. "How did she know he arrived here?"

He shrugged. "There's a lot more to Mrs. Hall than anyone knows. If she says she wants to meet him, we take him."

"Halloween is tomorrow." She laid her head on his shoulder. "Will you be able to perform your ritual with Wayne here? He won't upset the balance, will he? I mean if he really is Lily's child, could it pose a problem?"

He held her tight. "His presence doesn't change anything. All we need to do is find your grandmother's tree, and then I can perform the ritual to cross over the ghosts. It will all work out fine. Go on inside. I have to talk to Lucas."

As soon as she went in, Parker jumped in his truck and sped back to Lucas' shop. He screeched to a stop in front, barely getting the engine shut off before he jumped out. He wasn't surprised to see his mother's car and Mrs. Hall's car there, too. He hurried inside and joined the loose circle they stood in with Mrs. Hall at the center. They all turned to stare at him.

"The Huntsman is close," Mrs. Hall said. "I've clearly heard his hounds. They're much closer than they should be. The elders believe he's right outside the barrier around the town. I believe he'll arrive on Halloween night. If the past is any indication, I don't think our protections can stop him. He has the uncanny ability to find any weak spot in the barrier."

"I think you're right." He nodded. "I've felt it in the air. Lucas has, too. What do we do? We can't let him terrorize us like he's done before. And the ghosts are depending on me to help them cross over. I can't let him pull any more of them into his service."

"You won't." Sara draped her arm around his shoulders. "Your father is out with the mayor and the town elders to erect stronger barricades and wards. We're hoping those will help keep The Huntsman out. We've all sensed a different element involved this year."

Mrs. Hall stared at him. "What's going on at Dee's place? I've felt a shift in magic from there. I know there's a new arrival and told you I want him at the festival. Tell about him."

Parker looked at each one of them. "Renee's ex-boyfriend is here and from what he's said, we believe he might be Lily McGee's missing child."

"Then he's the catalyst drawing The Huntsman here. He didn't take him or his father when he came before. He destroyed Lily and left her in torment, longing for her family," Sara said. "Looks like I may need to update the history a little."

"I plan to speak with the young man tomorrow," Mrs. Hall said. "Lucas, you make sure all those plants of yours are beyond healthy. Feed them all the magic they can handle. We may need them sooner rather than later. Parker, you need to stay with Renee and keep an eye on her ex. The Huntsman could show up at any time. He's close, closer than he's been in the past thirty-five years. We all have jobs to do. I suggest we get to them."

****

"I don't want to go to any festival." Wayne threw his clothes in his suitcase. "You told me to leave, and that's what I plan to do."

"You are so stubborn, aren't you?" Renee glared at him. "Your presence has been requested at the Halloween festival. You'll go. End of story. I don't want to hear any more arguments."

He stopped packing and stared at her. "Why? Because you want me to see how happy you are with your new man? Thanks, but no thanks."

"Oh, good grief. That's not it at all." She forced herself not to shout and softened her voice. Now wasn't the time to lose her temper. "I want you to stay because you might be able to find out what your dad feared and what happened to your mom."

She could tell he mulled over what she'd told him. Wayne might be a lot of things, but stupid wasn't one of them. She needed to appeal to his logical side. He sat on the bed, a shirt dangling from his hands. Not only did she want to bring peace to Lily, but Wayne needed his own answers, even if he didn't know it yet.

"Will you go tomorrow?" she said. "Will you help me give peace to Lily McGee?"

His head snapped up, and he stared at her. "How did you know my mother's name?" He threw his shirt on the bed. "Fine. I'll attend the festival if there's any chance I can get answers."

He stomped out of his room and down the stairs. Renee blew out a breath as she followed him down to the foyer. Miss Dee came up behind her and patted her shoulder.

Renee glanced at her and then at Wayne, who sat, sulking, in one of the wingback chairs. "Well, that went about as well as could be expected. He's not happy with me or Garland Falls right now."

"Very true, dear. Very true. However, I believe this Halloween will see closure on many stories." Dee squeezed her shoulder. "Maybe I can help get him out of his bad mood. Leave him to me and my freshly baked cinnamon rolls. I had a feeling I might need extra today."

The door opened and Parker walked in. Renee's stomach clenched as the two men stared each other down. Parker turned to her. "Did you tell him to come to the festival tomorrow?"

"Yes. He's agreed to come." Renee frowned when Wayne snorted. "I think we need to take him to the north woods. Maybe Lily will come out when she sees him."

"It's possible. I think we should wait until tomorrow night when the new moon rises. I'll be at the top of my game and my power will strongest then. I'll be better able to protect him and the spirits who want to cross over."

"Wayne, I need you to wait here," Renee said. "Parker and I have to check an area out in the woods.

We'll be back soon. Whatever you do, don't go outside. Have Miss Dee give you something to eat. I highly recommend the cinnamon rolls."

Wayne stormed into the dining area where Dee had already placed a plate with two rolls on it in front of him. Renee grabbed her coat and followed Parker out to the porch.

"Do you think he'll want to come with us tomorrow?" Parker glanced back at the front door when they stood on the porch. "We really need him to be at the festival. Will he be okay?"

Renee glanced at the B and B, then smiled at him. "He's mad right now because he doesn't like all the changes happening to him. But yes, he'll be fine. I'm sure Miss Dee will get him to calm down. No one who eats her food can stay upset for very long." She sighed. "Especially when someone is given those awesome cinnamon rolls."

"I think you've developed an addiction to those," he said. "Let's get going. We have to get the area checked out. I hope The Huntsman hasn't been there yet."

"Same here."

They hurried toward the woods. Renee instinctively knew he would take her back to the fairy ring's clearing. There would be no stroll this time. Now, their steps were quick and their path sure as they rushed to where they needed to be. The whole time, Renee hoped the clearing would be free of The Huntsman's influence.

They burst into the clearing, and Renee stopped in front of the largest oak tree she'd ever seen in her life. It would take at least five people to circle the trunk.

Thick branches loomed overhead, blocking out the sun and sky. The branches were full of colorful autumn leaves and not one lay on the ground at its base. Birds sang from its leafy depths, giving the illusion the tree itself was singing.

"Wow. This is the hugest tree I've ever seen," she whispered.

Her grandmother floated behind her. "This is it, Renee. This is my tree. The fairy ring and the clearing look exactly like they did when your grandfather proposed to me here. Of course, the tree has grown quite a bit since that day."

Renee looked at Parker. "Gran says this is it. This is her tree."

"I heard her." Parker nodded. "I thought it would be. This is where I need to hold my ritual for the crossing."

"Do the fairies help you?"

"No. They don't like it when I the open gateway to the afterlife. That type of magic makes them skittish."

She smiled at him. "Well, lucky for you, I'm not a fairy. I'll help you in any way I can."

He pulled her close and kissed the top of her head. "Glad to hear it. I think you're the exact person I need to cross Lily over."

She crossed her fingers. "I hope I am. This whole family needs peace."

Chapter Fifteen

Parker mumbled as he tossed and turned in his sleep. A large shadow chased him through the woods, and he couldn't get away. The figure reached for him as he stumbled. He looked back…and sat straight up, a scream dying in his throat. He blinked several times and looked around his room. All was as it should be, or was it? Shadows held menace and familiar shapes took on a decidedly sinister air. He leaped out of bed and dived for the light switch beside the door. Light flooded the room and nothing menacing or sinister jumped out at him.

He sagged against the wall as the door opened slowly. He stumbled away, falling to the floor as Lucas stared at him. He dragged his hand across his forehead, wiping away the sweat beading there. He forced his breathing to slow, trying to get it back to normal.

"You okay, little bro?"

"Maybe?" Parker held his hand up and let Lucas pull him to his feet. "The Huntsman is close. I just had one heck of a nightmare, and he was in it. It was so real, like if he caught me, it would be all over. He'll be here on Halloween, just as we feared. We have to go check the woods at the edge of town. We may have to scope out near the B and B as well."

"I had the same nightmare. I came to see if you were all right." He paused. "Wait a minute. You want to check the woods for a huge, scary, supernatural being in the middle of the night?" When Parker nodded, he grinned. "Sounds like a good time. Let me get dressed."

Parker pulled on his clothes and prayed the dream wasn't a foretelling of bad things to come. If The Huntsman took his spirit in bondage, he wouldn't be able to help the ghosts around him. The spirits depended on him to help them cross over to the afterlife. The Huntsman would take all of them as his servants if Parker couldn't stop him and his hounds. He'd have to make sure all around him were safe at the ritual.

He hurried downstairs and shrugged into his jacket. Lucas tossed his keys to him. If he could possibly be in danger, what did that mean for Renee and her grandmother's ghost? Would he be strong enough to open the gateway and protect her and the spirits? He'd have to be because there wasn't any other choice. Guess he'd find out tomorrow night.

Lucas climbed into the passenger side of Parker's truck. They headed to the woods at the farthest point outside of town. Neither man spoke as the increasing heaviness in the air surrounded them. Parker slowed the truck and parked. He glanced at Lucas, and his brother nodded.

They got out and walked straight to the woods. A small fairy zoomed out and landed on Lucas' shoulder, hiding under his hair. All too soon, the sound they feared reached them. The Huntsman's hounds were here and howling in anticipation of the coming hunt. The ground trembled under their feet, a telling sign The Huntsman hadn't come alone.

"He's closer now than ever before," Parker said in a low voice. "Did you feel those tremors in the ground? He's on that monster of a horse of his."

"You heard how loud and how close the hounds are," Lucas said. "If that isn't a portent for disaster, I don't know what is. I hate to say it, but we have to go farther in to see what kind of havoc he's causing."

"Agreed."

They each took a deep breath and started for the dark, forested maw looming in front of them. They hadn't gone more than ten feet when the fairy on Lucas' shoulder began yanking on his hair. He held her in his hand. "I know you're afraid, but we need to scope out The Huntsman's position. I'll make sure you get safely home." He smiled. "You shouldn't have been out this late by yourself anyway. Keep yourself and your kin hidden until this is over."

They pushed deeper into the dense trees. Lucas knocked on a maple tree trunk, and a small doorway opened. He held his hand close to the door and the tiny fairy disappeared inside. The baying of the hounds grew louder the farther in they went. Parker held his arm out across Lucas' chest, stopping him from moving.

"Do you see them?" Parker whispered. "Over there to the right."

"I see them," Lucas whispered back. "Judging at how far those eyes are from the ground, I'd say the hounds have had a significant growth spurt in the last couple of decades."

"You're right." Parker watched as at least six pairs of blood-red eyes watched them. "I don't think Garland Falls is prepared for this. Should we push deeper to find out more?"

"I hate to say it, but yeah. I think we need to get as much information as we can. Besides, we aren't powerless. I mean we're surrounded by the nature our abilities are tied to. We can defend ourselves if we have to."

Parker glanced at him. "Let's hope we don't have to. Come on. We need to check out what's waiting for us."

"At least he only brought six hounds this time," Lucas said. "There's no way we'd have any kind of a chance to stop them if he'd brought the whole kennel."

"Big bro is right again. Let's find out what he wants."

The hounds kept pace with them as they pushed their way in through the thick brush, staying just out of sight. Every few minutes, they would bay and growl, or snap their teeth. The trees blocked the moonlight, closing over their heads in a thick cover, even though most of the branches were almost bare.

"Come no farther, Green Men," a deep voice said.

"Huntsman," Parker shouted. "We've come to ask you to stay away from Garland Falls. You have no business here and never did. Take your hounds and go."

Dark laughter surrounded them, making them stand close, back-to-back. An immense shadow pulled away from the trees and flowed toward them. "You do not give orders to The Huntsman, little man. The Hunt has gone on long before your time and will continue long after you are dust. Give me the spirit I crave, and I will leave your town in peace. Deny me, and there will be consequences."

Parker faced the Huntsman's shadow, and his

brother's hand landed on his shoulder. "The spirits here, all the spirits are under my protection. I will deny you, Huntsman. Everyone, living or dead, will be safe from becoming your servants."

"Then, Green Man, you have made a bad choice. Tomorrow night, I shall appear, and I shall take my due."

The Huntsman's shadow loomed larger over the brothers. He brought his shadow hand down, forcing them to their knees. They struggled to rise but couldn't. The hounds moved in closer, so close Parker and Lucas could smell the fetid stench of their hot breath. The Huntsman stepped closer, stopping right in front of them.

"I listened to the petition of the Green Prince once before. He pleaded your case, and I allowed you to leave our realm and live among the humans." He leaned close. "In your time here on the mortal world, you have forgotten how to show your liege the respect he deserves. I will come for both of you. And you shall not like your fate when I return you to our lands."

"And we are grateful for your generosity," Parker said, struggling to raise his head, the muscles in his neck tightening. "But we still intend to stop you from hurting any of the spirits or living people we are sworn to protect. In this, we are forced to deny you. We apologize, but we cannot change any of our future actions against you."

"Then I pity you, Green Man, and your kin. Be warned. When next we meet, you will feel my wrath at your defiance."

The Huntsman melted back into the darkness around them, and they watched the hounds back away until they could no longer be seen or heard. The brothers looked at each other and rose to their feet. In silent agreement, they turned and hurried out of the woods. They no longer needed to check the area around Miss Dee's place. They had found out everything they needed to know right here.

In the truck, Parker was silent as he drove them home. He was grateful Lucas knew him well enough to not say a word until he felt ready to speak. He parked in his spot behind their house and sat there, listening to the ticking engine as it cooled.

"I'm in way over my head this year." He glanced at Lucas. "I don't know if I'll be powerful enough to stop him. I don't think he remembers why we left his realm in the first place. Mom and Dad were fed up with his ridiculous rules. We were lucky we had the Green Prince on our side then, and hopefully now, too."

"I'd love for Mom to talk to The Huntsman. I don't think he scares her as much as he thinks he does. The elders should be able to protect you." Lucas grinned. "I'm pretty sure Renee will stand by you and help any way she can. Now is not the time for your faith in your abilities or the people around you to falter. You got this, little bro. My plants and I will lend more power to the earth. You'll have all the help we can give you."

"Thanks, big bro. I may need every ounce of it."

****

Renee sat straight up in bed, her chest heaving. "Gran, are you here?"

Her grandmother appeared next to her. "I sensed you had trouble sleeping so I stayed with you. What's the matter?"

"I don't know. I have an awful feeling Parker's in

danger and there's nothing I can do." She jumped out of bed and threw her robe on. "I need to check on Wayne. He might be feeling this, too."

She hurried down to his room and just as she was about to knock, the door flew open. Wayne stood there, his hair mussed and a wild gleam in his eyes. "I was just coming to find you. I had a horrible nightmare."

"So did I. Let's go downstairs and I'll make us some tea."

They walked into the dining room and Dee was already there with a pot of tea, three cups, and a plate of biscuits. "I take it you sensed the darkness, too?"

Renee and Wayne looked at each other. "We both had nightmares," she said. "There's something big going on, isn't there?"

"Yes." Dee busied herself with pouring tea for the three of them. "This may be the most important Halloween ever. Events are in motion and gaining speed every hour."

Dee waited until they sat down and placed the cups in front of them. "Tomorrow night is Halloween. Renee, you, Wayne, and Parker will face a dangerous foe called The Huntsman. He wants what he believes to be his and won't be swayed. The three of you will have to be stronger than you've ever been before. You'll need to call on your power more than you have in the past, Renee." She squeezed her hand. "Don't worry. You'll have all the help you'll need."

Wayne looked at the two women. "I don't understand. What do you mean?"

Dee patted his hand. "Garland Falls is many things to many people, but the one thing it always is, is magical. That element which draws good people also draws the bad. Wayne, you may have come here for Renee, but I fear you will leave with more answers about her and who you are than you ever wanted to know."

"Miss Dee," Renee said slowly. "Will Parker be safe when he performs the ritual tomorrow night?"

Dee finally smiled. "Of course. You'll be there to protect him, and you'll have your part to play too, Wayne." She stood. "Finish your tea and go back to bed. Halloween will arrive before we know it, and you two must be ready. Get some rest."

They drained their cups and stood. "Good night, Miss Dee," Renee said, and Wayne nodded.

Chapter Sixteen

Halloween dawned bright and clear. The wind stilled, as though it seemed to feel the tension surrounding the town. The brothers ate breakfast in silence. As they washed the dishes and put them away, Renee's grandmother appeared in their kitchen. She smiled at both of them and gave them a thumbs up. When she disappeared, they grabbed their jackets and left.

They looked at each other as they stood in front of their house. "This is the calm before the storm," Parker said. "The Huntsman and his hounds will make it through the barriers and wards. When they do, I'm afraid I won't be strong enough to stop him. The Huntsman doesn't give up on his prey without a fight." He unlocked his truck's driver side door. "And he threatened to return us to the fairy realm."

"Don't I know it, and I have no desire to go back there." Lucas couldn't help but glance at the woods at the edge of his fields. He handed a large bundle of flowers to his brother. "I wish Blair was here. She'd be a big help."

"I know, but there's nothing we can do about it," Parker said, taking the bundle from Lucas. "It'll be a clear night for the ritual. I can feel my power getting stronger as the day goes on."

Lucas glanced at him. "You worried about

tonight?"

"More than I should be." He loaded the bundle into the bed of his truck. "I feel like the air around me is weighing me down, and tonight it might be worse. When The Huntsman shows, the spirits will run. I don't want him to trap any more of them in servitude to him. I'd like to free the ones he's already enslaved."

"Good luck with that plan." Lucas pushed his hat back and stared at the sky. "Mrs. Hall and the elders have done everything they could to protect the town. We're as ready as we'll ever be. You still sure this Wayne guy might be the answer?"

"Yep. I think The Huntsman has come specifically for him since he didn't get him or his parents before. Renee said his father had nightmares about being hunted. It's possible The Huntsman collected his spirit when he passed away." Parker kicked at a loose rock on the driveway, sending it skittering toward the grass. "I hope we can keep Wayne safe."

"We can, and we will. I'm sure of it." Lucas smiled and nodded. "I'm glad Renee's grandmother gave us her approval."

Parker grinned. "I already had her approval. I think it was more for you than me. She still thinks you're pushy, though." He turned serious. "We'd better get ready for tonight. We've only got fourteen hours to prepare, and we'll need every minute. Lucas," he said. "Would the Green Prince intercede for us again if we called on him?"

"I don't know, little bro, but I doubt it. We needed Mom to browbeat him into helping us before. He tries to keep a low profile around our 'liege,' remember?"

"I remember. Good thing we have the elders to

help. See you at the festival."

Lucas walked to his shop and opened the back door. Parker took another look at the clear sky and climbed in his truck. Time to get to Miss Dee's and collect Renee and Wayne. He wanted them where he could keep an eye on them. There was so much riding on the ritual this year, more than any other since he'd taken over helping the spirits.

He took a deep breath and let it out slowly. The sky might be clear, but The Huntsman and his hounds had muddied everything about today and tonight. The ritual was about a rebirth for the soul. The spirits who sought him out should feel safe while he opened the gateway to the afterlife. He shouldn't have to worry about some spectral fairy king with a bad attitude. He turned the key and the truck rumbled to life. Time to go to the Halloween festival and pretend everything would work out fine.

****

"Wayne, why do you have to be such a pain?" Renee asked. "Just get ready. You're going to the festival, whether you like it or not. Didn't the nightmare help you decide this is what you need to do? Now get a move on."

He stared at her. "You've never spoken to me like this in all the time we've been together. What's changed you?"

"I think it's because we don't have to tiptoe around each other any longer. We've made the right decision to break up. I never wanted to hurt you." She squeezed his hand. "You have to admit, it feels pretty good to know we no longer have to pretend or force feelings that aren't there."

He grinned. "It does. It hurt at first, but then I realized you were right. We had been going through the motions of a relationship. I hope you'll be happy here with Parker." He held his hand out. "Friends?"

"Friends." She kissed his cheek. "And I know I'll be happy with Parker. Now, let's get this mess settled. He'll tell us what he wants us to do and when. I still need to spread Gran's ashes, but now I know where."

Wayne kept ahold of her hand as they sat on the couch. "You've said some odd things since I came here. What did Miss Dee mean about your power? What exactly can you do? Are you like one of those flashy superheroes in the movies? I'd like to try to understand."

"No, I'm not flashy, nothing like that." Renee took a deep breath. "I have the ability to see and talk to ghosts. There's plenty of them in this town. Parker can do it, too. He helps spirits cross over to the other side. He says he's a spirit conduit."

He squeezed her hand. "I knew you were a special lady, and I'm sure you'll fit in here just fine. The people of Garland Falls are lucky to have you."

"You're taking this awfully well." She stared at him. "You're not surprised or freaked out?"

"Oh, I'm totally freaked out. It's not something you hear every day." He walked to the window and stared out. "But if your new guy can accept it, I guess I can, too. From what you said, he does the same thing you do." He smiled at her. "As an executive, I've learned how to get unexpected news and not lose my composure."

"And you're a great executive. I'm sure you'll find an equally great lady who's just perfect for you." She headed for the stairs. "Let's get ready for the festival. Parker will be here any time now to pick us up."

"You believe he's Lily's son?" Gran asked as soon as she appeared in the room.

Renee pulled a sweater over her head and flipped her hair out. "I do. It's the only explanation that fits with all he told me."

Gran floated in front of her. "It sure sounds like it to me." She paused. "Wayne took your breakup well."

"He didn't at first, but he soon realized I was right." She tugged a brush through her hair and turned to her grandmother. "When you cross over, I'll miss you, Gran. You've been so supportive of me. I know you need to go, but sometimes, I don't want you to."

"I know. I'll miss you, too, dear, but I'll look out for you from the other side." Gran smiled. "Now that you've embraced your gift, you might be able to hear me every so often."

"I hope so." Renee took a deep breath to stop the tears threatening to spill and changed the subject. "I think I heard Parker's truck pull up. I'd better get down there."

She knocked on Wayne's door and there was no answer. He must have already gone downstairs. She hurried down the steps and found Parker in the drawing room. She looked around. "Where's Wayne?"

"He isn't with you?"

She shook her head. "I went to get ready and I thought he did, too." They hurried to the kitchen. "Miss Dee, have you seen Wayne?"

"I believe he stepped outside for a few minutes."

Renee and Parker looked at each other. "I didn't see him when I drove up," he said.

"Oh no. You don't think he would've gone into the north woods alone, do you?" Parker's silence confirmed her fears. "We've got to find him."

"If that's where he went, something or someone drew him there." He held her coat for her. "Don't worry. The Huntsman won't show until tonight. He's usually weak in the daylight. Wayne should be safe for now, but I'd rather not take a chance. The Huntsman's power has grown, so I'm not sure if he's contained to only wander the night hours any longer."

They hurried out and into the woods. He held his hand up, and she stopped. Leaves crunched off to their right, the sound echoing in the silent woods. They headed in that direction, stopping to listen for any other noise.

Parker glanced at her and gave a small nod of his head. "Call him. Maybe he can lead us to where he is."

"Wayne," she called out. "You need to come back now. Parker's here, and we have to leave. Mrs. Hall wants to meet you."

They stood still and a quiet groan drifted to them on the breeze. He led them off to the left. They found Wayne sitting on a fallen log as he rubbed his head. Parker pulled him to his feet while Renee stared at his eyes.

"Wayne, what happened?" she asked.

"I'm not sure. While I waited for you to come down, I heard this voice. It wanted me to come to the woods. When I got here, something didn't feel right. I started back to the B and B, but I got turned around." He rubbed the back of his neck. "I started to run, and I tripped over a rock or a log. Before I knew it, a huge, black shape loomed over me. It looked like a man, but it had horns or antlers or something bizarre on the top of his head. I thought I heard a woman's voice, too. She told the horned guy to leave me alone."

"That's not good. The Huntsman is closer than he should be and shouldn't have been able to manifest, even his voice, in the daylight. I knew he'd gotten stronger, but I didn't realize how much. I thought we'd have until the time for the ritual before he showed." Parker glanced at Renee, then Wayne. "Come on. Let's get you back to the B and B."

"Sounds like a great idea," Wayne said.

Parker pulled his arm over his shoulders. Renee took his other arm, and they helped him back to Miss Dee's. "You need to get cleaned up so we can get you to the festival."

Wayne groaned. "I don't think I'm up for a party."

"You don't have a choice," Renee said. "Being at the festival with us is the safest place for you right now. The black shape you saw is The Huntsman, and he has come back specifically for you."

They made it out of the woods and crossed the lawn. "Of course he has," Wayne grumbled.

"Don't worry," Parker said. "We won't let him get you."

"I hope you're right."

Wayne went up to his room to clean up while Renee and Parker waited for him in the drawing room. "Parker," Renee said slowly. "Do you think it was Lily who saved Wayne?"

"I'm sure of it." He glanced up at the ceiling. "I think she suspects he's her son. If true, we have a powerful ally against The Huntsman tonight."

She stepped close to him and sighed when his arm went around her shoulders. "I hope so. I think we're going to need all the help we can get."

Chapter Seventeen

The three of them arrived at the Halloween festival in the town hall just after noon. Children laughed and ran around, weaving in and out of the crowd. A food table had been set up along the far wall. People participated in all sorts of crafts and games. In the middle of it all, Mrs. Hall barked orders, checked on supplies, and smoothed out any rough spots. Parker waved to her, and she hurried over.

"So this is our guest," she said. She held his hands and smiled at him. "Welcome to Garland Falls, Wayne. We're so happy you could join us."

"Thank you. I'm glad you invited me."

Mrs. Hall peered at him. "You look exactly like your mother."

"Wait. You knew her? Did you know my dad, too?"

She nodded. "Your mother was a lovely, frail girl. We could never understand what she saw in Edmund McGee."

"Mrs. Hall," he said. "There's no way my dad would've hurt her. Until the day he died, he said that over and over. Whatever the people here thought of him, he'd never hurt anyone. He loved my mom. He showed me some old photos of the two of them. If you could see them, how he looked at her, you'd know he could never hurt her. He adored her."

Parker's mother approached them. "I see you made it."

"Mrs. Callahan, this is my friend, Wayne Billings," Renee said. "Wayne, this is Sara Callahan, Parker's mother."

Sara stared at Wayne. "Your mother's maiden name was Billings. Did your father change your last name when the two of you left?"

"Billings is the only name I've ever known." He looked at the people who surrounded him. "My dad never explained why he had a different last name from mine."

"I bet he wanted to protect you from The Huntsman," Parker said. "If all of this is true, we expect The Huntsman to show up tonight to try and claim you. I'm expecting him to come to the ritual site."

Wayne sighed and stared at the ceiling. "I should've stayed in New York."

Parker laid his hand on Wayne's shoulder. "Where you lived wouldn't have made any difference. If The Huntsman wants you, he'll find you."

Wayne frowned at him. "Don't you ever have any good news for me?"

****

Lucas pulled Parker aside. "The air has gotten more oppressive. The Huntsman is almost here for Renee's friend. How do you plan we should stop him?"

"Get the elders. They can set up a defensive wall." Parker glanced at Renee as she talked with Mrs. Hall and his mother. "Renee might be able to help me with the ritual. Her abilities are similar to mine and almost as strong. If we can cross over Lily, The Huntsman may lose some of his power."

"That's a mighty big 'if,' little bro. What happens if you can't?"

Parker gave him a small grin. "Then, I guess we're all doomed. The Huntsman and his hounds will run over this town and take all the spirits with him. We'll be headed back to the fairy realm for his weird brand of justice for defying him. After all, he could feed off our power for decades. I don't think the Green Prince would appreciate us messing up what he did for our family in the past. After all, he risked a lot for us back then."

"You're a real barrel of laughs sometimes, you know that, Parker?"

"Yep."

Renee approached them. "Can you guys feel something bad coming?"

"We were just talking about it," Parker said, and Lucas nodded.

"We have to take Wayne with us to the woods for the ritual, don't we?" she asked. "I feel in my gut it's the right way to go."

Parker nodded. "Me, too. It'll put him in jeopardy, but he'll draw out Lily. Maybe she can help us stop The Huntsman."

"It's a chance we'll have to take." She paused. "Before we go to the ritual site, I need to go the B and B to get Gran's urn. Can't spread the ashes if I don't have them."

"Very true."

She smiled and pulled him toward one of the craft tables. "Well, until we go out in a fiery blaze of glory, we might as well have some fun."

Parker loved her enthusiasm as she made a

Halloween mask and a scarecrow. Soon, she dragged him over to play some of the games that were set up. They filled up on the different foods and snacks. The time flew and before long the town clock struck eleven. The new moon cast a dark shadow over the town as its white ring shone brightly around it.

Parents herded their children out the door to get them tucked into their beds. As people drifted out, they wished Parker, Renee, and Wayne luck. Everyone in town had some sense of the high stakes this holiday. Lucas hugged his brother and headed back to his fields. He'd promised to draw on the power of nature to feed into Parker's.

Renee walked over to Wayne. "We have to go. You need to come out to the woods with us tonight. I won't lie. This will be dangerous for you. The Huntsman wants you, but we mean to stop him."

"Great," Wayne said. "Like I said to Parker, don't you ever have any good news for me?"

"Your mother's spirit should come out to protect you."

He shrugged. "I'll take it. You think she'll be at peace after tonight?"

"I believe so," Parker said. "She's waited a long time for you to return. She'll want to see you. I think you're the last piece of her puzzle. We believe it was her spirit who helped you this morning."

The three of them left and headed for the B and B. The two men waited in the foyer while Renee ran to her room and grabbed the urn. She turned and smiled at her grandmother over her shoulder before heading back downstairs.

"Gran, are you coming with us? After all, you need

to be at the clearing for the ritual to cross you over to the afterlife."

"I'll be beside you the whole time. Let's get this done."

Renee took a deep breath and hurried down to meet the two men waiting for her. She gripped the urn tighter to her chest as they walked toward the north woods. The closer they got, the heavier the air got around them. Even the ghosts who followed them felt it. Some faded from sight, while others stayed with them.

"It's so hard to breathe." Wayne's steps faltered and he slowed down a little. "I don't think I can do this."

"Yes, you can. You're stronger than you think." Renee laid her hand on his arm. "It's okay. Parker and I will protect you. You won't have to worry about The Huntsman after tonight." She smiled. "And your dad will have justification that he really did love your mother and you."

"I hope you're right."

Parker hushed them as they followed him into the woods. He cradled the floral bundle he'd picked up from Lucas in his left arm. In his right hand he carried a small burlap sack. The trees seemed to close in around them, their steps muffled by the carpet of leaves. The deeper they went, the more a great sadness enveloped them.

"Call your mother," Parker whispered.

Wayne glanced at him. "Are you sure?"

"I can't cross her over unless she's here. Let her know who you are and that you've come back. Tell her you're safe and you're here to help her." He nodded and gave him a small smile. "It's okay. She loves you.

She has no reason to harm you."

"If you say so." Wayne took a deep breath and stepped away from Parker and Renee. "Lily McGee? It's me. It's your son, Wayne. I've come back to tell you I'm safe and unharmed. You need to come out and let Parker help you cross over. It's okay. You don't need to stay here any longer."

The trees bent as a stiff wind blew around them. Leaves and dirt swirled up around their faces, making them cover their eyes. Soon, a pale figure materialized before them. Wayne jumped behind Renee when the ghostly woman reached her hand out.

"It's all right," Renee said. "It's Lily. Go to her."

Wayne stepped out and walked toward the ghost. "Mom, is it you?" She nodded and her fingers caressed his cheek, making him shiver at the cold contact. "You know Dad never hurt you, right?" She nodded again. "I've missed you all of my life."

"I always prayed your father had kept you safe," she said, her musical voice soft. "I'm so happy to see you doing so well. I've missed you so much these many, long years."

"Dad never stopped loving you." Wayne held his hand out and she laid her ghostly one in his. "He felt so guilty he couldn't keep you safe."

A trumpet sounded in the distance, a familiar cadence of calling hounds to the hunt. Faint at first, it grew louder by the minute, followed by the sound of baying hounds and pounding hooves. All conversation stopped and the three of them turned as one. Lily's eyes widened and her head snapped around and she ran through the trees, fading with every step.

"Mom, don't go," Wayne shouted. "We're here to

help you. We can keep you safe."

"Come on," Parker said. "We've got to get to the ritual site. The Huntsman will be here quicker than we want. We've got to get started."

They hurried to the curtain of vines and Parker shoved it aside, gesturing for the other two go in first. He removed his shoes and stopped at the fairy ring first. He opened the sack and set out a small bottle of wine, some bread and cheese, and seven gold coins. Power surged into the soles of his feet, and he knew Lucas had begun his own incantations. The smell of the woods filled him, and he held his hands up calling more of the power of nature into himself.

He thanked the fairies for their permission to use their sacred circle. He offered the gifts on the ground as a thank you for their blessing. He unrolled the bundle and began to place flowers in a circle at the base of the oak tree. He started with a dark red rose, then a dark pink geranium, a pale pink peony, a bright yellow daffodil, working through a rainbow of colors, all the way to the last flower in his hands. Even though some of the flowers were out of season, Lucas had provided all the needed blooms from his greenhouse.

He held a large white gardenia with reverence, bowing his head over it. When the circle was complete except for one last spot, he circled the oak tree again, murmuring a quiet incantation. The trumpet grew louder, and the hounds sounded closer than ever. His hands shook, but he didn't stop. The ritual needed to be complete to open the door to the afterlife. The Huntsman would have to take a back seat to the spirits depending on him.

"Parker, you have to hurry," Renee whispered, her

voice shaking. "He's almost here."

He nodded in silent acknowledgement, never taking his gaze from the ring of blossoms. He raised the gardenia up to the new moon, letting the dark, blue sphere and white ring of light shine on it. With the incantation completed, he lowered it, and bowed his head. "As I place this last bloom, the spiritual connection will be complete. Let the scent of this gardenia open the gateway to the other side. Let the spirits who are here find peace in the afterlife."

As he laid the white flower at the top of the circle, every flower glowed with ethereal light. The Huntsman burst into the clearing, his blood-red eyes boring into them. Astride his huge, pitch-black horse, they couldn't tell where the horse ended and his body began. He dismounted and stalked toward them, making them all back away. Parker stood straighter, summoning whatever inner strength he could. The spirits needed him, now more than ever.

The Huntsman could easily be ten feet tall, if not more. His dark tan pants and tattered shirt had the distinct sound and smell of well-oiled leather. A long, black cape fluttered around his legs as he got closer to the small group. Black boots ended halfway up his thighs, his footsteps sending shockwaves through the ground, while his hounds circled on huge paws, snapping at the small group when they got close.

His skin was deep brown and rough, like the bark of a tree. Long, moss-green hair flowed from under the helmet covering most of his face. The head-dress itself was frightening, with a jagged edge resembling sharp teeth. What they initially thought were horns curving from the top of the helmet were more like antlers. Small prongs jutted out all the way up and the top points appeared thick and sharp. His eyes glared at them from underneath the head covering, flaring with malice.

"Green Man, you will give me the spirit who has eluded me for far too long," he said, his hollow voice reverberating through their skulls. "This will be your last chance for leniency from me. Do not forget the warning I gave you the previous night."

Parker bowed to him in a show of respect. "Forgive me, Huntsman, but I can't let you harm any of the spirits here, living or dead. I have pledged to keep them safe until they cross over to their well-earned rest. You need to return to the realm of fairy. You have no chance at taking this man or any spirit from this sacred place."

The hounds circled Parker and Wayne, snarling as saliva dripped from their massive jowls. Renee started toward him, but he shook his head and held his hand up, stopping her. The hounds jumped at him, their teeth snapping inches from his fingers.

"Finish the ritual," he called out.

"I don't know how," she cried.

Wayne stepped forward and brandished a large branch he'd picked up. "We've got this, Renee. Do what you need to do." He turned his attention to The Huntsman. "You took my mother from me. You haunted my father's dreams until he died. You won't hurt me or anyone else."

The Huntsman leaned close. "You were chosen to be mine, boy. This is a high honor for you. Come with me now and I'll spare the others."

"Thanks, but I'm afraid it's an honor I'll have to do without." He hefted the branch a little higher on his shoulder. "You should listen to Parker and go back to wherever it is you came from."

"You have no idea how this honor was bestowed on you, do you?" The Huntsman laughed, a sound chilling them all. "Your father's village offered himself and his firstborn to me to keep them all safe from my hunt."

"Well, then they didn't really know my father," Wayne spat out. "He wouldn't have gone along with that plan, not by any stretch of the imagination."

"How little you know of your heritage, boy. The villagers did, but you're right. Your father ran off with you." He leaned down close to Wayne's face. "The bargain was struck, and it is your duty, your obligation, to honor it."

Parker stepped in front of him. "No deal, Huntsman. I am a descendant of the Green Prince, as are my brother and parents. Even though you rule over us, we have the power to stop you. There won't be any spirits for you here this year or any other. The bargain you speak of will not be honored in the mortal realm. This man is free from the deal you struck. I'll use every power at my disposal to stop you, here and now."

"Are you so sure, so confident, in your words, Green Man? Let's test that, shall we?"

The Huntsman reached out with his power. Green cords of light wrapped around Wayne's body, drawing his spirit out of him. His back arched and his grip on the branch loosened when The Huntsman gave a hard yank. Wayne grimaced and fought to pull his spirit back into his physical body.

Parker immediately countered with a blue light cord, anchoring Wayne's ghostly self with his physical form. The ghost of Lily McGee reared up out of the ground and stepped in front of them, blocking The Huntsman's way to her son. She used herself as a shield, stopping The Huntsman's attempts to steal Wayne's spirit. Parker grabbed Wayne's hand and murmured a short incantation. The blue cord turned into a silver thread, linking him, Wayne, and Lily in an unbreakable chain. A powerful barrier formed around them, glowing bright and strong. The Huntsman continued tugging on Wayne's spirit, and the green cord around Wayne couldn't be broken.

The Huntsman swung his thick arm, knocking Parker to the side. He rolled and pushed to his feet. He wrapped the silver thread tighter around his fingers and stared defiantly at the large entity towering over them. He felt blood trickle down his cheek and narrowed his eyes. Liege or not, The Huntsman had just overstepped his bounds.

"This is my clearing to perform the sacred ritual, giving peace to the spirits who come to me," Parker shouted. "I won't let you soil the rites to be said in this place of peace. You'll take no spirits from here this year."

The Huntsman lashed out again, knocking Parker off his feet for a second time. He staggered back over to Wayne and strengthened the thread between them. He'd told Wayne he'd protect him, and he meant to keep that promise, no matter what. He grabbed the silver thread and wrapped it tighter around his fist, keeping Wayne anchored solidly to his body.

Wayne stepped in front of him and swung the branch, connecting with one of the hounds. He brought it down again and the hound yelped as it scrambled backwards. As the others continued to circle, he swung the branch in a wide arc, keeping them back as he made his way over to Parker, when The Huntsman knocked him down for a third time. Parker shook his head, blinking rapidly to clear his vision. He took Wayne's extended his hand, letting him pull him to his feet.

"Are you all right?" Wayne asked. "That's a pretty nasty cut."

"I'm good, but if we can't stop The Huntsman soon, it will be the least of my problems." Parker stepped next to him and nodded as Wayne gripped his makeshift weapon tighter. "Leave now, Huntsman. All in this glade are under my protection. I'll fight you with everything I have to stop you."

"And he won't fight you alone," Wayne said.

The Huntsman laughed. "I know how much power is within you, Green Man. You cannot match me in that regard." He lashed out again, and Wayne was dragged closer to him as his spirit was tied to The Huntsman's horse, the silver thread Parker had conjured thinning. "I will have this boy and there's nothing you can do. As my subject, my will is yours. Do not expect the Green Prince to interfere on your behalf this time. He has slunk back to his pitiful castle on the outskirts of my lands."

"I'm not now, nor have I ever been, your subject, and I don't need the Green Prince's help to defeat you now," Parker shouted. "My parents left your realm. You have no claim on me or anyone here in Garland Falls, including the man standing here."

The Huntsman grew taller and pointed at him. "Insolent boy. It appears a lesson needs to be taught." The hounds surrounded his legs, waiting for a command to attack. "Not yet, my pets, not yet. Obey my orders, Green Man. This is your last chance. You have no choice but to bow to my will."

"I can't and I don't want any of your chances." Parker stood straighter, refusing to avert his gaze. "You've hurt too many people and ghosts through the years. I'll do anything and everything I can to stop you. Right here and right now."

"So be it."

Parker watched The Huntsman drag his finger through the air and his chest burned. He refused to give in to the pain filling him and pulled more of Lucas' power into himself. The burning ceased and he strengthened his grip on the silver thread. It was more important than ever to keep Wayne and Lily safe.

"Renee, you have to finish the ritual," he yelled. "If not, there'll be no stopping The Huntsman. All the spirits need you, need your strength. *I* need you."

"I'll try, but I've never done anything like this before."

"You can do this." He blocked another attack from The Huntsman. "Just believe in your power."

He spared her a quick glance to see her hurry over to the oak tree and set her grandmother's urn on the ground. He blocked another attack from The Huntsman. She had to finish the ritual and she had to do it soon. If not, everyone and every ghost didn't stand a chance against The Huntsman and his hounds.

Lily's ghost faded in and out. Wayne's skin was beginning to pale the longer The Huntsman had his spectral rope around him. When the branch Wayne held fell to the ground, Parker realized his strength was waning fast. Renee needed to hurry. They were in a literal fight for everyone's life.

Chapter Eighteen

Renee stared at the ring of flowers and didn't have a clue on how to proceed. She wanted Parker to come over and finish the ritual, but he was a little busy right now. She talked to ghosts, but she couldn't help them cross over. Could she? He was depending on her, they all were, and she didn't know what to do next. She had to try and pray she didn't screw up what he'd started. She clenched her fists, then flexed her fingers, and wished she had Parker's experience.

"Renee, you know what to do," Gran whispered when she materialized. "Look inside yourself. The knowledge is there. You have to find it. You have to believe in your skills."

"I'm scared I'll mess it up, Gran. I need Parker's help. I've never even thought about attempting anything like this before. I've never even heard of anything like this before." She turned to her grandmother's ghost. "What do I do?"

Gran looked over her shoulder. "You'd better do something or Parker and Wayne and everyone else are done for. Come on, girl. Get yourself together. You have the instinct to know what to do. Use your gift."

Renee looked at The Huntsman as he loomed over the two men in her life and Lily's ghost. The three of them were in deep trouble if she didn't do something soon. Gran was right, as always. She needed to focus on her ability and help the spirits, Parker, and Wayne. She glanced behind her and watched as Parker stood in front of Wayne, shielding him from The Huntsman's wrath. He wove his arms in elaborate patterns, and bright blue light surrounded them. She could see a silver thread tied around him, Wayne, and Lily.

The Huntsman's horse glared at her and snorted. As she stared at the massive beast, she saw a large sack tied to the saddle's pommel and something inside was struggling to get out. That had to be the spirits he'd captured. They needed to be freed, so they too, could cross over to the afterlife. She had to do what she could for them. Determination made her stand taller. Gran was right again. Everyone in the clearing needed her to be stronger than she'd ever been in her life.

"Focus, Renee. People are depending on you," she muttered.

Would Parker's power be strong enough to delay The Huntsman and his hounds? When Wayne swung the branch he held, a little bit of pride puffed up in her chest. She didn't think he had it in him. She cringed when she saw The Huntsman knock Parker to the ground and then scratch his chest without ever touching him. This entity was really powerful and Parker, along with Wayne, depended on her to help stop him.

The best way to do that was to finish a ritual she'd never done or heard of until she came to Garland Falls. Parker had erected some kind of a magical shield around them. For now, it seemed to keep The Huntsman's hounds at bay. What would happen if the hounds decided to come for her? Could she be as strong as the two men behind her? There wasn't any choice. She'd have to be.

She cringed as the hounds leapt at the barrier, scratching and gnawing as they tried to get in. The Huntsman smashed his large fists down and the blue dome faltered for a moment. Parker dropped to one knee and stretched his arms out. The shield glowed brighter and pushed out against the attack. Wayne grabbed Parker under his arms and hauled him to his feet. The Huntsman bellowed and lowered his massive fists again and she took a step toward them.

"Finish the ritual," Parker shouted. "The ghosts are depending on you to open the gateway."

"I don't know how," she cried.

"Yes, you do. You know you can do it."

Her head whipped back and forth between them and the ghosts hovering in the trees. She closed her eyes and concentrated on her power. She laid her hand on the gardenia. Golden light surrounded her, and the earth thrummed under her feet. She kicked her shoes off and let the power of the surrounding trees and all of nature in the clearing fill her. Energy rose up within her, and a deep connection bound her to every living and un-living being around her.

She opened up her abilities and felt an instant connection to the spirits hovering away from The Huntsman and his hounds. They flowed to her side, and she stood, calling more to her. Power surged into her and a light beyond the veil began to shine brightly, making her squint. She raised her arms, her fingers weaving in a strange pattern of their own accord. In the middle of the circle, a doorway opened and revealed a bright, colorful passageway. A gasp escaped her at the warmth and beauty flowing out of the gate.

Her power sang within her and called out to all the

spirits in the area. The Huntsman roared as ghosts zoomed in from every direction, flying past him and filling the clearing. Occupied with trying to break Parker's protection spell, he couldn't turn his attention to capture any of them. One by one, they sailed through the doorway and were swallowed by the light. She backed up until she was right by the large sack.

The horse whipped its head around and snapped at her. "I don't think so," she said, bringing her palm down hard on its nose. "Bad horse. Mind your manners."

When it reared back in surprise, she yanked on the rope and the sack opened. Spirits shot out in all directions, heading for the opening to the afterlife. The Huntsman roared, shaking the trees, and turned to her. When his attention was diverted, Parker sent out a thread to hold him in place. She nodded at him and concentrated on keeping the portal open.

Renee's grandmother floated next to her and smiled. "I'm so proud of you, my dear. I knew you had it in you. You've always been filled with magic. Being in Garland Falls has awakened it and brought it up to its full potential. You truly belong here."

"Thanks, Gran. That means a lot." Her breath hitched and she swallowed hard. "I know you have to go, but I don't want you to. I don't know how I'll get along without you." Tears streamed down Renee's cheeks as her grandmother floated surrounded by the light. "I'll miss you so much, Gran."

"You'll figure it out. I'll miss you, too, my dear." Her grandmother gave her a hug that chilled her blood. "I'm waiting for my old man to come for me." She peered into the light. "There he is now. He never could be on time. Remember, I'll always be with you. Now go help your men out. I'll take care of the ghosts."

As Gran directed the spirits into the gateway, Renee walked over to Parker and grabbed his hand. The silver thread flowed around her, connecting her to the other three, glowing brightly. It regained its strength, growing back to its original thickness.

"You need to leave, Huntsman," she shouted. "There is no place for you here. Take your hounds and go."

The Huntsman loomed over her, if possible getting even taller. "Who are you to speak to me in such a way, girl? Do you not realize I can destroy you? You are but a mere mortal and not worthy to address me in such a way."

"Apparently, I'm more than human, and even if I am a 'mere mortal,' this is my world. You can try to destroy me, but you can't touch me, and you know it. I'm not part of your realm and therefore you have no claim on me, nor do I have to listen to anything you say." Renee raised her chin in defiance of the shaking her knees were doing. "I'm a protector of spirits and a conduit for them to the afterlife. You can't win this time. Make it easy on everyone and leave."

The Huntsman pointed to Wayne. "I'll have this man as payment. The man who sired him stole him away, though I finally took him in servitude in place of what I was owed. The woman who gave him life escaped me, but he will not. Give him and the woman to me now and you shall all be spared my wrath."

Lily's ghost stretched until she stood as tall as him. "You took my life when my husband tried to save me and our child. You won't harm my son, and you will never make me serve you. If it takes eternity, I will fight you and free any spirits you bind in servitude."

A man's spirit floated over to where the stood. "You have kept me captive long enough, Huntsman. I'm with my family and you can't divide us again, no matter how hard you try."

"Dad?" Wayne whispered.

Wayne's father and mother joined hands, blocking any access to Wayne that The Huntsman tried to get. He stood with them, the silver thread linking the whole group, living and ghost, to Parker. The more people who joined in the protection spell, the stronger it became. The hounds backed away, snarling in fear. Even The Huntsman's horse shied away as the three living and two ghosts glowed with power.

"I have told of the bargain struck with this man's village. He and his offspring are owed to me. Green Man, you defy me at your peril."

"Oh, grow up," Renee said. She cast out her own silver thread, connecting it with Parker's. "You sound like a whiny, spoiled brat. So, like a brat, why don't you take your toys and go home?"

Renee grinned at the shocked look on Parker's and Wayne's faces. Who knew she'd have the courage to stand up to a being who could squish her with one blow? A large group of people came through the woods and formed a circle in the clearing. She smiled at the crowd before focusing again on the gateway, keeping it open.

More spirits were filling the clearing, heading straight for the gateway ahead of the crowd. Thank goodness the cavalry had arrived. About time, too. Leading the charge were Miss Dee and Mrs. Hall. Of course, those two lively ladies would be at the forefront.

"Back up a little," Mrs. Hall shouted. "We'll put this party crasher in his place. Come on, everyone, let's get this done."

Miss Dee and Mrs. Hall led the town elders in casting a banishment spell. The stood in a loose circle around The Huntsman, his horse, and his hounds and linked hands. As they shouted the spell in unison, glowing purple sigils formed in the air. Behind them, the fairy ring glowed pink and the mushrooms expanded to twice their normal size.

As the runes surrounded The Huntsman, he howled his rage. His hounds yelped and his horse reared up as a cyclone enveloped them all before it shrank down to a pinpoint and winked out. When the wind stopped, The Huntsman, his horse, and his hounds were nowhere to be found.

"I'm so glad to see you again, Lily," Wayne's father said. "I regretted for the rest of my life I couldn't save you."

"I know, my dear," Lily said, as she laid her hand on Wayne's cheek. "You loved us more than anyone in Garland Falls knew."

Wayne nodded. "I knew. I've always known."

Lily smiled. "You have magic in you, too." She turned to her husband. "Would you like to tell him?"

He nodded. "My parents were from a part of the fairy realm known as the Dark Lands. I'm actually an ogre. My tribe made me, and by association my folks, outcasts because we didn't look like the rest of the ogres in our village. I could pass for human. My parents couldn't, but I could. When it was time for me to leave home, I wandered over to the realm's Light Side and met your mother. Her lineage is leprechaun, and one of the more powerful families." He smiled at her. "We fell in love and, despite everyone condemning us, we got married. We were forced to leave the fairy realm, so we settled here, in Garland Falls."

His mother took over. "We weren't sure if we'd be accepted here, so we lived outside of town and kept to ourselves." She smiled at Mrs. Hall and the elders. "I suppose we should've asked for help, but we'd had such bad luck with other people. We were afraid of letting others know our secret."

Wayne looked at his hands. "So I'm part ogre and part leprechaun? That explains how I knew to swing that branch and connect in the right spot." He smiled when she nodded. "I guess that's what also makes me good at my job as an accountant. I just can't take no for an answer when talking to new clients." He gazed at his parents. "Are you sure you have to leave? I've wanted the three of us to be together all my life."

"I'm sorry. I've waited for so many years to have the answers denied me in life." Lily smiled. "Now that I've found you and know what a fine young man you turned out to be, it's time for me to go. I've waited so long to be with your father again." She gazed at her husband. "I'm happy to be reunited with him. I've missed you both so much. Take care, my baby boy. We shall always love you, and we'll be watching out for you from the other side."

Wayne's father shook his hand, sending chills running down his spine. "Thank you, son. I always wanted to tell you how much I appreciated your help while I was alive. You're a good man."

"Thanks, Dad. I love you guys."

They all watched as his parents drifted toward the passageway. They paused and smiled at him one more time before smiling at each other. They turned and waved before joining hands and disappearing inside. As soon as they were gone, the light faded. Parker wrapped his arms around Renee. Wayne was surrounded by the elders and hugged by Mrs. Hall.

"Let's head to the Bed and Breakfast," Miss Dee said. "I'll make some tea and put out some food. We all need to replenish our strength. This has been a most tiring evening."

One by one, the small crowd talked in low voices as they drifted out of the woods. As soon as they were alone, Renee opened the urn and spread her grandmother's ashes all around the base of the tree. The flowers glowed with a brilliant white light for a moment, which then faded away.

"Goodbye, Gran," she said, tears running freely down her cheeks. "Hug Gramps for me. I love you guys."

Parker helped Renee to her feet and brushed the tears from her eyes. "Looks like you're a spirit conduit after all," he said. "And it appears that you might be from a magical realm yourself."

"Well, I've heard anything's possible in Garland Falls."

"I can't believe you called The Huntsman a spoiled brat." He held her close. "No wonder my mother likes you so much."

"I can't believe I did it either." She wrapped her arms around his waist. "He just made me so mad, I had to say something."

"I completely understand." He kissed the top of her head. "I'm glad you're on our side."

She laid her hand on the tree and bowed her head for a moment, then picked up her grandmother's now empty urn. "Let's get back to the B and B." She shivered and hugged herself, while slipping her shoes on. "It's way too cold to stand around out here. I think my toes are frozen. You know, I thought after I spread Gran's ashes, I'd be totally alone."

"And now?"

She laid her head on his shoulder as he held her close. "Now I know I'll never be alone as long as I have you."

"Then you'll never be alone."

When they walked in, Dee gave them each a cup of hot chamomile tea and a small plate with several cookies on it. They didn't see Wayne with the group at the table. Dee glanced upward, telling them he'd gone to his room. The rest of the elders sat at the dining room table and talked in quiet voices while they drank from mugs. Renee and Parker sat on the loveseat in the drawing room.

Parker glanced up. "Will he be okay?"

"Wayne?" She nodded. "He'll be all right. He needs time to process what happened tonight. You know, for him being half ogre and half leprechaun, he's actually a pretty decent guy. It explains a lot about his personality. I'm glad we found out the truth about Lily and her husband with the town elders there."

"Same here." He grabbed a cookie from the plate. "Now my mother can update the story of Lily McGee and give her the happy ending the whole family deserves."

She sipped her tea. "I'll have to go back with him, you know. I've got to pack my stuff and close my business. I've also got to get Gran's house on the market. There's a million things I have to take care of back east."

"Oh." He squirmed on the loveseat. "Should I go with you?"

She chuckled. "As much as you dislike cities? I don't think so. Besides, I need you here."

"Why?"

"You really are a man of few words." She finished her tea and snuggled close to him, sighing when his arm went around her shoulders. "I leased a store on Main Street. When I send my stock here, I need someone to take it to the shop for me. I need a place to live, too. I'd appreciate it if you'd take care of everything on this end." She sat up and raised her hand to her chest in mock surprise. "You didn't expect me to do it all by myself, did you?"

"I guess not." He pulled her back down to his side. "All right. I'll get your place of business and a house for you set up. Thanks for trusting my judgement with something so important." He kissed the top of her head. "I'll miss you."

"You're welcome, and it won't take me long." She frowned a little. "At least I hope it won't. With paperwork, you just never know, and don't worry. I'll be back before you know it."

He held her tightly. "I hope so. I'm tired of dealing with Lucas by myself. I'll be glad when his wife gets home."

She snuggled close to him. "Don't worry. I'll give you so much to do, you won't have time to miss me or deal with Lucas."

Chapter Nineteen

Parker unloaded another delivery from Renee into her new store. He didn't realize she'd have so much merchandise. She must love her work to be so prolific with her stock. He opened the boxes and sorted the items in the back room. Who knew you could have so many styles of belts and bags?

He held one up. She was incredibly talented with a needle. The design work itself must have taken her at least a week to do. Some of the gloves she'd made were fleece lined and had been sewn with small, delicate stitches. Others had small beads stitched to them. Still others looked more like driving gloves.

He'd drafted Lucas to help him, and they had cleaned the store, built shelves in the back, and put the front counters together. They stocked the shelves, set several displays, and hung purses, bags, and hats. He adjusted some watercolor paintings he'd bought from a local artist. He hoped he hadn't overstepped his bounds and Renee would like what they'd done.

He'd found a perfect house for her the next street over from Main Street with the money she left him to purchase one if he found the perfect place. A small two-story home, white with blue shutters, just perfect for her. She had a small, fenced in yard in the front and back, with plenty of room for a garden. He couldn't wait to help her start planting different flowers. He was sure Lucas would make some great decisions on what would look the best. He was anxious to show her Callahan's Floral Emporium and let her start planning what she would plant in the spring.

Maybe one day they'd get married and he'd move in with her. Then he could be out of Lucas' house, especially since his brother had gotten himself a wife of his own. No matter how much they said they loved having him there, he always felt like a third wheel. He was sure they'd want to have some time to themselves.

"I knew you'd have it worse than me when you found the right woman," Lucas said when he stopped in. "And I believe I told you that some time ago. If I recall, you said I was crazy."

Parker frowned at him. "Don't you have flower arrangements to put together?"

"And give up the chance to needle you while we have the time?" He grinned. "I let Ray take over for me while I'm here. Seriously though, I think Renee is your perfect match. You also called me crazy when I told you I believed in perfect matches."

"You're right about two things. She is my perfect match, and I still think you're crazy." He finally stared at Lucas. "I'm sorry I ever doubted you, big bro. I can't believe I found her."

"And that she decided to stay here with you." Lucas grabbed him in a quick hug. "I'm happy for both of you."

"Thanks again. Mom will be happy to know I've finally found a love of my own." Parker squeezed his brother's shoulder. "Enough of this. We should get back to work."

They worked together to finish unloading the boxes

and storing the overstock in the storeroom. They broke down the cartons and took them out back to the dumpster. Back inside, Parker grabbed the broom and swept up the remaining dust and pieces of packing material. His brother whistled while he cleaned the glass counter tops.

"Renee have any idea when she'll be back?" Lucas finally asked. "I know Blair will love her, and she gets home from her current assignment next week. I can't wait for the two of them to meet."

"Wayne shipped all of her personal belongings and I got the last of the boxes a few days ago." Parker put the broom away. "She said it didn't take long to find a buyer for her grandmother's house, but she's buried in paperwork. I guess it's not as easy to move a business. She also said this shipment from her store was the last one."

"I guess paperwork will be the downfall of us all. I'm glad there aren't any more boxes coming. We're almost out of room." Lucas threw the rag in a bucket and walked to the door. "Come on. Let's get some food. My treat."

They walked out and Parker locked the door. He stared at store front and hoped Renee would like the sign he and Lucas had made. If not, he'd take it down and do it again. Her happiness, and nothing else, was all that mattered.

****

Renee walked into Warner's B and B and dropped her suitcase on the floor. Dee came out of the dining room and hurried over to grab her in a tight hug. "My dear, it's so good to see you again. I'm glad you made it back before winter set in. Are you here for good?"

Renee smiled. "For good. Garland Falls is now officially my home. I hope Parker found me somewhere to live. As much as I love being here with you, I'd like to have my own place."

Dee's eyes sparkled with delight. "I think he found you the perfect house. He'll be around tomorrow to show you."

"I'm right here, Miss Dee," Parker said from the foyer. "I've picked up a sixth sense where Ms. Tate is concerned. I knew she'd be here today."

Renee turned and threw herself into his arms. "I missed you so much. I hated it took so long for me to get all the paperwork settled. I almost came back before I had it all finished."

"I'm glad you got it done." He held her close. "I missed you a lot, too. What I said was true. I sensed when you got into town, and Lucas said his flowers knew when you arrived. Are you tired? Do you want to go get something to eat?"

"I'm exhausted, but I would love some food. I'm starving." She turned to Dee. "I'll be back later. Then, I think I might sleep for three days. Maybe more."

"Have fun, you two," Dee said. "I'll see you tomorrow, Renee. Parker, don't be late for work in the morning."

"I'm never late, Miss Dee. You know that." The two of them laughed as they left the B and B. He leaned close and whispered in her ear. "Like I told you the first week you were here, I set my own hours, so I can't be late."

"Mr. Callahan, that's what's known as an incredibly large loophole."

Parker held the truck door open, and Renee

climbed in. "Are you okay with a small side trip before we eat?"

"Sure. Of course, it might cost you a bigger dinner."

"Deal. Close your eyes." He parked in front of her new shop and hurried around to help her out. He stood behind her and laid his hands on her shoulders. "Okay, now look."

She blinked several times when she opened her eyes. Painted on the window in blue and gold read "Renee's Creative Leather Gifts." He'd already set a beautiful display of belts, gloves, and messenger bags in the window. He'd posted a big "Coming Soon" sign on the door.

"Oh, Parker, it's beautiful."

"We've already had a lot of people asking when you were going to be open. I didn't give them a date because I wasn't sure if you wanted to have a grand opening event." He unlocked the door and led her inside, then handed her the keys. "Lucas and I built you some counters out here and you have shelves in your back room."

He showed her an area at the back of the store, facing the door. "We made this spot a work space for you. This way, you can create out here where people can see what you do. We wanted to let you fill it with your tools and things."

She threw her arms around his neck and hugged him tight. "You're the best man I've ever met. I love it." She gazed at him. "I love you."

"I love you, too." He kissed her. "I bought you a house on the next street over. Do you think maybe, one day, we'd live there together?"

"Parker Callahan, did you propose to me after just knowing me for a couple of weeks?"

"Yeah. I guess so." He grinned. "And because I want to move out of Lucas' house. It's too crowded there now."

She traced his jaw. "I knew you had to have another reason. However, you can't take it back, so I accept."

"Good."

They locked up her store and walked to the diner. Two people who could talk to ghosts in one town. She suspected they'd have a very spirited romance for the rest of their lives. And she was fine with that.

A word about the author…

I graduated from Mercy High in Baltimore, MD in 1981 and got married to an Air Force man in 1982. We have two amazing boys who have grown into amazing young men. We spent sixteen years in southern New Jersey, four of them at McGuire AFB and the rest in Hammonton. We currently live in Memphis, TN where science fiction, wrestling, and hockey take up what time the cat doesn't.

www.annettemillerauthor.com